ENCHANTRESS OF VENUS

AN ERIC JOHN STARK
ADVENTURE

BY

LEIGH BRACKETT

VERT VOLTA PRESS
REDISCOVERY
Edition

Book and Cover Design: Vladimir Verano, VertVolta Design

ISBN: 978-1-60944-107-4

VertVolta Press

vvdesignpress@gmail.com

www.vertvoltapress.com

BETA

Anya

Breksta Dorsa

E V E R E

Mons

da
er ×VENERA-9

Truth

Jászai
Patera

ZEMIRE
CORONA

P L A N I T I A

RENENTI
CORONA

Barton
Lachappelle

PURANDHI
CORONA

Zorile Dorsa

HINDLA REGIO

Aurelia

Sif Mons
2km

Gul
3km

×VENERA-10

Seymour

HILDA CORONA

Tuli
Mons

Cunitz

UNDINE PLANITIA

Vakarine Vallis

Mortim-Ekva
Fluctus

Heng-o Cha

HENG-O
CORONA

300°

320°

340°

DOLYA
TESSERA

NAVKA PLANITIA

×VENERA-13

KANYKEY
PLANITIA

×VENERA-14

Bender

RASSA PLANITIA

IWERIDD
CORONA

QETESH
CORONA

LIBAN FARRA

Carson

Ushas
Mons

Aglaonice
Danilova

Samundra
Vallis

Saskia

DIONE

Innini
Mons

COF

Tefnut
Mons

REGIO

ZYWIE
CORONA

Hather
Mons

HEMIS REGIO

LAVINA PLANITIA

KIBU-FATMA

I

THE SHIP MOVED SLOWLY ACROSS THE RED SEA, THROUGH THE shrouding veils of mist, her sail barely filled by the languid thrust of the wind. Her hull, of a thin light metal, floated without sound, the surface of the strange ocean parting before her prow in silent rippling streamers of flame.

Night deepened toward the ship, a river of indigo flowing out of the west. The man known as Stark stood alone by the after rail and watched its coming. He was full of impatience and a gathering sense of danger, so that it seemed to him that even the hot wind smelled of it.

The steersman lay drowsily over his sweep. He was a big man, with skin and hair the color of milk. He did not speak, but Stark felt that now and again the man's eyes turned toward him, pale and calculating under half-closed lids, with a secret avarice.

The captain and the two other members of the little coasting vessel's crew were forward, at their evening meal. Once or twice Stark heard a burst of laughter, half-whispered and furtive. It was as though all four shared in some private joke, from which he was rigidly excluded.

The heat was oppressive. Sweat gathered on Stark's dark face. His shirt stuck to his back. The air was heavy with moisture, tainted with the muddy fecundity of the land that brooded westward behind the eternal fog.

There was something ominous about the sea itself. Even on its own world, the Red Sea is hardly more than legend. It lies behind the Mountains of White Cloud, the great barrier wall that hides away half a planet. Few men have gone beyond that barrier, into the vast mystery of Inner Venus. Fewer still have come back.

Stark was one of that handful. Three times before he had crossed the mountains, and once he had stayed for nearly a year. But he had never quite grown used to the Red Sea.

It was not water. It was gaseous, dense enough to float the buoyant hulls of the metal ships, and it burned perpetually with its deep inner fires. The mists that clouded it were stained with the bloody glow. Beneath the surface Stark could see the drifts of flame where the lazy currents ran, and the little coiling bursts of sparks that came upward and spread and melted into other bursts, so that the face of the sea was like a cosmos of crimson stars.

It was very beautiful, glowing against the blue, luminous darkness of the night. Beautiful, and strange.

There was a padding of bare feet, and the captain, Malthor, came up to Stark, his outlines dim and ghostly in the gloom.

"We will reach Shuruun," he said, "before the second glass is run."

Stark nodded. "Good."

The voyage had seemed endless, and the close confinement of the narrow deck had got badly on his nerves.

"You will like Shuruun," said the captain jovially. "Our wine, our food, our women—all superb. We don't have many visitors. We keep to ourselves, as you will see. But those who do come…"

He laughed, and clapped Stark on the shoulder. "Ah, yes. You will be happy in Shuruun!"

It seemed to Stark that he caught an echo of laughter from the unseen crew, as though they listened and found a hidden jest in Malthor's words.

Stark said, "That's fine."

"Perhaps," said Malthor, "you would like to lodge with me. I could make you a good price."

He had made a good price for Stark's passage from up the coast. An exorbitantly good one.

Stark said, "No."

"You don't have to be afraid," said the Venusian, in a confidential tone. "The strangers who come to Shuruun all have the same reason. It's a good place to hide. We're out of everybody's reach."

He paused, but Stark did not rise to his bait. Presently he chuckled and went on, "In fact, it's such a safe place that most of the strangers decide to stay on. Now, at my house, I could give you..."

Stark said again, flatly, "No."

The captain shrugged. "Very well. Think it over, anyway." He peered ahead into the red, coiling mists. "Ah! See there?" He pointed, and Stark made out the shadowy loom of cliffs. "We are coming into the strait now."

Malthor turned and took the steering sweep himself, the helmsman going forward to join the others. The ship began to pick up speed. Stark saw that she had come into the grip of a current that swept toward the cliffs, a river of fire racing ever more swiftly in the depths of the sea.

The dark wall seemed to plunge toward them. At first Stark could see no passage. Then, suddenly, a narrow crimson streak appeared, widened, and became a gut of boiling flame, rushing silently around broken rocks. Red fog rose like smoke. The ship quivered, sprang ahead, and tore like a mad thing into the heart of the inferno.

In spite of himself, Stark's hands tightened on the rail. Tattered veils of mist swirled past them. The sea, the air, the ship itself, seemed drenched in blood. There was no sound, in all that wild sweep of current through the strait Only the sullen fires burst and flowed.

The reflected glare showed Stark that the Straits of Shuruun were defended. Squat fortresses brooded on the cliffs. There were ballistas, and great windlasses for the drawing of nets across the narrow throat.

The men of Shuruun could enforce their law that barred all foreign shipping from their gulf.

They had reason for such a law, and such a defense. The legitimate trade of Shuruun, such as it was, was in wine and the delicate laces woven from spider-silk. Actually, however, the city lived and throve on piracy, the arts of wrecking, and a contraband trade in the distilled juice of the vela poppy.

Looking at the rocks and the fortresses, Stark could understand how it was that Shuruun had been able for more centuries than anyone could tell to victimize the shipping of the Red Sea, and offer a refuge to the outlaw, the wolf's-head, the breaker of taboo.

With startling abruptness, they were through the gut and drifting on the still surface of this all but landlocked arm of the Red Sea.

Because of the shrouding fog, Stark could see nothing of the land. But the smell of it was stronger, warm damp soil and the heavy, faintly rotten perfume of vegetation half jungle, half swamp. Once, through a rift in the wreathing vapor, he thought he glimpsed the shadowy bulk of an island, but it was gone at once.

After the terrifying rush of the strait, it seemed to Stark that the ship barely moved. His impatience and the subtle sense of danger deepened. He began to pace the deck, with the nervous, velvet motion of a prowling cat. The moist, steamy air seemed all but unbreathable after the clean dryness of Mars, from whence he had come so recently. It was oppressively still.

Suddenly he stopped, his head thrown back, listening.

The sound was borne faintly on the slow wind. It came from everywhere and nowhere, a vague dim thing without source or direction. It almost seemed that the night itself had spoken—the hot blue night of Venus, crying out of the mists with a tongue of infinite woe.

It faded and died away, only half heard, leaving behind it a sense of aching sadness, as though all the misery and longing of a world had found voice in that desolate wail.

Stark shivered. For a time there was silence, and then he heard the sound again, now on a deeper note. Still faint and far away, it was sustained longer by the vagaries of the heavy air, and it became a chant, rising and falling. There were no words. It was not the sort of thing that would have need of words. Then it was gone again.

Stark turned to Malthor. "What was that?"

The man looked at him curiously. He seemed not to have heard.

"That wailing sound," said Stark impatiently.

"Oh, that." The Venusian shrugged. "A trick of the wind. It sighs in the hollow rocks around the strait."

He yawned, giving place again to the steersman, and came to stand beside Stark. The Earthman ignored him. For some reason, that sound half heard through the mists had brought his uneasiness to a sharp pitch.

Civilization had brushed over Stark with a light hand. Raised from infancy by half-human aboriginals, his perceptions were still those of a savage. His ear was good.

Malthor lied. That cry of pain was not made by any wind.

"I have known several Earthmen," said Malthor, changing the subject, but not too swiftly. "None of them were like you."

Intuition warned Stark to play along. "I don't come from Earth," he said. "I come from Mercury."

Malthor puzzled over that. Venus is a cloudy world, where no man has ever seen the Sun, let alone a star. The captain had heard vaguely of these things. Earth and Mars he knew of. But Mercury was an unknown word.

Stark explained. "The planet nearest the Sun. It's very hot there. The Sun blazes like a huge fire, and there are no clouds to shield it."

"Ah. That is why your skin is so dark." He held his own pale fore-arm close to Stark's and shook his head. "I have never seen such skin," he said admiringly. "Nor such great muscles."

Looking up, he went on in a tone of complete friendliness, "I wish you would stay with me. You'll find no better lodgings in Shuru-un. And I warn you, there are people in the town who will take advantage of strangers—rob them, even slay them. Now, I am known by all as a man of honor. You could sleep soundly under my roof."

He paused, then added with a smile, "Also, I have a daughter. An excellent cook—and very beautiful."

The woeful chanting came again, dim and distant on the wind, an echo of warning against some unimagined fate.

Stark said for the third time, "No."

He needed no intuition to tell him to walk wide of the captain. The man was a rogue, and not a very subtle one.

A flint-hard, angry look came briefly into Malthor's eyes. "You're a stubborn man. You'll find that Shuruun is no place for stubbornness."

He turned and went away. Stark remained where he was. The ship drifted on through a slow eternity of time. And all down that long still gulf of the Red Sea, through the heat and the wreathing fog, the ghostly chanting haunted him, like the keening of lost souls in some forgotten hell.

Presently the course of the ship was altered. Malthor came again to the afterdeck, giving a few quiet commands. Stark saw land ahead, a darker blur on the night, and then the shrouded outlines of a city.

Torches blazed on the quays and in the streets, and the low buildings caught a ruddy glow from the burning sea itself. A squat and ugly town, Shuruun, crouching witch-like on the rocky shore, her ragged skirts dipped in blood.

The ship drifted in toward the quays.

Stark heard a whisper of movement behind him, the hushed and purposeful padding of naked feet. He turned, with the astonishing swiftness of an animal that feels itself threatened, his hand dropping to his gun.

A belaying pin, thrown by the steersman, struck the side of his head with stunning force. Reeling, half blinded, he saw the distorted shapes of men closing in upon him. Malthor's voice sounded, low and hard. A second belaying pin whizzed through the air and cracked against Stark's shoulder.

Hands were laid upon him. Bodies, heavy and strong, bore his down. Malthor laughed.

Stark's teeth glinted bare and white. Someone's cheek brushed past, and he sank them into the flesh. He began to growl, a sound that should never have come from a human throat. It seemed to the startled Venusians that the man they had attacked had by some wizardry become a beast, at the first touch of violence.

The man with the torn cheek screamed. There was a voiceless scuffling on the deck, a terrible intensity of motion, and then the great dark body rose and shook itself free of the tangle, and was gone, over the rail, leaving Malthor with nothing but the silken rags of a shirt in his hands.

The surface of the Red Sea closed without a ripple over Stark. There was a burst of crimson sparks, a momentary trail of flame going down like a drowned comet, and then—nothing.

II

STARK DROPPED SLOWLY DOWNWARD THROUGH A STRANGE world. There was no difficulty about breathing, as in a sea of water. The gases of the Red Sea support life quite well, and the creatures that dwell in it have almost normal lungs.

Stark did not pay much attention at first, except to keep his balance automatically. He was still dazed from the blow, and he was raging with anger and pain.

The primitive in him, whose name was not Stark but N'Chaka, and who had fought and starved and hunted in the blazing valleys of Mercury's Twilight Belt, learning lessons he never forgot, wished to return and slay Malthor and his men. He regretted that he had not torn out their throats, for now his trail would never be safe from them.

But the man Stark, who had learned some more bitter lessons in the name of civilization, knew the unwisdom of that. He snarled over his aching head, and cursed the Venusians in the harsh, crude dialect that was his mother tongue, but he did not turn back. There would be time enough for Malthor.

It struck him that the gulf was very deep.

Fighting down his rage, he began to swim in the direction of the shore. There was no sign of pursuit, and he judged that Malthor had decided to let him go. He puzzled over the reason for the attack. It could hardly be robbery, since he carried nothing but the clothes he stood in, and very little money.

No. There was some deeper reason. A reason connected with Malthor's insistence that he lodge with him. Stark smiled. It was not a pleasant smile. He was thinking of Shuruun, and the things men said about it, around the shores of the Red Sea.

Then his face hardened. The dim coiling fires through which he swam brought him memories of other times he had gone adventuring in the depths of the Red Sea.

He had not been alone then. Helvi had gone with him—the tall son of a barbarian kinglet up-coast by Yarell. They had hunted strange beasts through the crystal forests of the sea-bottom and bathed in the welling flames that pulse from the very heart of Venus to feed the ocean. They had been brothers.

Now Helvi was gone, into Shuruun. He had never returned.

Stark swam on. And presently he saw below him in the red gloom something that made him drop lower, frowning with surprise.

There were trees beneath him. Great forest giants towering up into an eerie sky, their branches swaying gently to the slow wash of the currents.

Stark was puzzled. The forests where he and Helvi had hunted were truly crystalline, without even the memory of life. The "trees" were no more trees in actuality than the branching corals of Terra's southern oceans.

But these were real, or had been. He thought at first that they still lived, for their leaves were green, and here and there creepers had starred them with great nodding blossoms of gold and purple and waxy white. But when he floated down close enough to touch them, he realized that they were dead—trees, creepers, blossoms, all.

They had not mummified, nor turned to stone. They were pliable, and their colors were very bright. Simply, they had ceased to live, and the gases of the sea had preserved them by some chemical magic, so perfectly that barely a leaf had fallen.

Stark did not venture into the shadowy denseness below the topmost branches. A strange fear came over him, at the sight of that vast forest dreaming in the depths of the gulf, drowned and forgotten, as though wondering why the birds had gone, taking with them the warm rains and the light of day.

He thrust his way upward, himself like a huge dark bird above the branches. An overwhelming impulse to get away from that unearthly place drove him on, his half-wild sense shuddering with an impression of evil so great that it took all his acquired common-sense to assure him that he was not pursued by demons.

He broke the surface at last, to find that he had lost his direction in the red deep and made a long circle around, so that he was far below Shuruun. He made his way back, not hurrying now, and presently clambered out over the black rocks.

He stood at the end of a muddy lane that wandered in toward the town. He followed it, moving neither fast nor slow, but with a wary alertness.

Huts of wattle-and-daub took shape out of the fog, increased in numbers, became a street of dwellings. Here and there rush-lights glimmered through the slitted windows. A man and a woman clung together in a low doorway. They saw him and sprang apart, and the woman gave a little cry. Stark went on. He did not look back, but he knew that they were following him quietly, at a little distance.

The lane twisted snakelike upon itself, crawling now through a crowded jumble of houses. There were more lights, and more people, tall white-skinned folk of the swamp-edges, with pale eyes and long hair the color of new flax, and the faces of wolves.

Stark passed among them, alien and strange with his black hair and sun-darkened skin. They did not speak, nor try to stop him. Only they looked at him out of the red fog, with a curious blend of amusement and fear, and some of them followed him, keeping well behind. A gang of small naked children came from somewhere among the houses and ran shouting beside him, out of reach, until one boy threw a stone and screamed something unintelligible except for one word—Lhari. Then they all stopped, horrified, and fled.

Stark went on, through the quarter of the lacemakers, heading by instinct toward the wharves. The glow of the Red Sea pervaded all the air, so that it seemed as though the mist was full of tiny drops of blood. There was a smell about the place he did not like, a damp miasma of mud and crowding bodies and wine, and the breath of the vela poppy. Shuruun was an unclean town, and it stank of evil.

There was something else about it, a subtle thing that touched Stark's nerves with a chill finger. Fear. He could see the shadow of it in the eyes of the people, hear its undertone in their voices. The wolves of Shuruun did not feel safe in their own kennel. Unconsciously, as this feeling grew upon him, Stark's step grew more and more wary, his eyes more cold and hard.

He came out into a broad square by the harbor front. He could see the ghostly ships moored along the quays, the piled casks of wine, the tangle of masts and cordage dim against the background of the burning gulf. There were many torches here. Large low buildings stood around the square. There was laughter and the sound of voices from the dark verandas, and somewhere a woman sang to the melancholy lilting of a reed pipe.

A suffused glow of light in the distance ahead caught Stark's eye. That way the streets sloped to a higher ground, and straining his vision against the fog, he made out very dimly the tall bulk of a castle crouched on the low cliffs, looking with bright eyes upon the night, and the streets of Shuruun.

Stark hesitated briefly. Then he started across the square toward the largest of the taverns.

There were a number of people in the open space, mostly sailors and their women. They were loose and foolish with wine, but even so they stopped where they were and stared at the dark stranger, and then drew back from him, still staring.

Those who had followed Stark came into the square after him and then paused, spreading out in an aimless sort of way to join with other groups, whispering among themselves.

The woman stopped singing in the middle of a phrase.

A curious silence fell on the square. A nervous sibilance ran round and round under the silence, and men came slowly out from the verandas and the doors of the wine shops. Suddenly a woman with disheveled hair pointed her arm at Stark and laughed, the shrieking laugh of a harpy.

Stark found his way barred by three tall young men with hard mouths and crafty eyes, who smiled at him as hounds smile before the kill.

"Stranger," they said. "Earthman."

"Outlaw," answered Stark, and it was only half a lie.

One of the young men took a step forward. "Did you fly like a dragon over the Mountains of White Cloud? Did you drop from the sky?"

"I came on Malthor's ship."

A kind of sigh went round the square, and with it the name of Malthor. The eager faces of the young men grew heavy with disappointment. But the leader said sharply, "I was on the quay when Malthor docked. You were not on board."

It was Stark's turn to smile. In the light of the torches, his eyes blazed cold and bright as ice against the sun.

"Ask Malthor the reason for that," he said. "Ask the man with the torn cheek. Or perhaps," he added softly, "you would like to learn for yourselves."

The young men looked at him, scowling, in an odd mood of indecision. Stark settled himself, every muscle loose and ready. And the woman who had laughed crept closer and peered at Stark through her tangled hair, breathing heavily of the poppy wine.

All at once she said loudly, "He came out of the sea. That's where he came from. He's..."

One of the young men struck her across the mouth and she fell down in the mud. A burly seaman ran out and caught her by the hair, dragging her to her feet again. His face was frightened and very angry. He hauled the woman away, cursing her for a fool and beating her as he went. She spat out blood, and said no more.

"Well," said Stark to the young men. "Have you made up your minds?"

"Minds!" said a voice behind them—a harsh-timbered, rasping voice that handled the liquid vocables of the Venusian speech very clumsily indeed. "They have no minds, these whelps! If they had, they'd be off about their business, instead of standing here badgering a stranger."

The young men turned, and now between them Stark could see the man who had spoken. He stood on the steps of the tavern. He was an Earthman, and at first Stark thought he was old, because his hair was white and his face deeply lined. His body was wasted with fever, the muscles all gone to knotty strings twisted over bone. He leaned heavily on a stick, and one leg was crooked and terribly scarred.

He grinned at Stark and said, in colloquial English, "Watch me get rid of 'em!"

He began to tongue-lash the young men, telling them that they were idiots, the misbegotten offspring of swamp-toads, utterly without manners, and that if they did not believe the stranger's story they should go and ask Malthor, as he suggested. Finally he shook his stick at them, fairly screeching.

"Go on, now. Go away! Leave us alone—my brother of Earth and I!"

The young men gave one hesitant glance at Stark's feral eyes. Then they looked at each other and shrugged, and went away across the square half sheepishly, like great loutish boys caught in some misdemeanor.

The white-haired Earthman beckoned to Stark. And, as Stark came up to him on the steps he said under his breath, almost angrily, "You're in a trap."

Stark glanced back over his shoulder. At the edge of the square the three young men had met a fourth, who had his face bound up in a rag. They vanished almost at once into a side street, but not before Stark had recognized the fourth man as Malthor.

It was the captain he had branded.

With loud cheerfulness, the lame man said in Venusian, "Come in and drink with me, brother, and we will talk of Earth."

III

THE TAVERN WAS OF THE STANDARD LOW-CLASS VENUSIAN pattern—a single huge room under bare thatch, the wall half open with the reed shutters rolled up, the floor of split logs propped up on piling out of the mud. A long low bar, little tables, mangy skins and heaps of dubious cushions on the floor around them, and at one end the entertainers—two old men with a drum and a reed pipe, and a couple of sulky, tired-looking girls.

The lame man led Stark to a table in the corner and sank down, calling for wine. His eyes, which were dark and haunted by long pain, burned with excitement. His hands shook. Before Stark had sat down he had begun to talk, his words stumbling over themselves as though he could not get them out fast enough.

"How is it there now? Has it changed any? Tell me how it is— the cities, the lights, the paved streets, the women, the Sun. Oh Lord, what I wouldn't give to see the Sun again, and women with dark hair and their clothes on!" He leaned forward, staring hungrily into Stark's face, as though he could see those things mirrored there. "For God's sake, talk to me—talk to me in English, and tell me about Earth!"

"How long have you been here?" asked Stark.

"I don't know. How do you reckon time on a world without a Sun, without one damned little star to look at? Ten years, a hundred years, how should I know? Forever. Tell me about Earth."

Stark smiled wryly. "I haven't been there for a long time. The police were too ready with a welcoming committee. But the last time I saw it, it was just the same."

The lame man shivered. He was not looking at Stark now, but at some place far beyond him.

"Autumn woods," he said. "Red and gold on the brown hills. Snow. I can remember how it felt to be cold. The air bit you when you breathed it. And the women wore high-heeled slippers. No big bare feet tromping in the mud, but little sharp heels tapping on clean pavement."

Suddenly he glared at Stark, his eyes furious and bright with tears.

"Why the hell did you have to come here and start me remembering? I'm Larrabee. I live in Shuruun. I've been here forever, and I'll be here till I die. There isn't any Earth. It's gone. Just look up into the sky, and you'll know it's gone. There's nothing anywhere but clouds, and Venus, and mud."

He sat still, shaking, turning his head from side to side. A man came with wine, put it down, and went away again. The tavern was very quiet. There was a wide space empty around the two Earthmen. Beyond that people lay on the cushions, sipping the poppy wine and watching with a sort of furtive expectancy.

Abruptly, Larrabee laughed, a harsh sound that held a certain honest mirth.

"I don't know why I should get sentimental about Earth at this late date. Never thought much about it when I was there."

Nevertheless, he kept his gaze averted, and when he picked up his cup his hand trembled so that he spilled some of the wine.

Stark was staring at him in unbelief. "Larrabee," he said. "You're Mike Larrabee. You're the man who got half a million credits out of the strong room of the Royal Venus."

Larrabee nodded. "And got away with it, right over the Mountains of White Cloud, that they said couldn't be flown. And do you know where that half a million is now? At the bottom of the Red Sea, along with my ship and my crew, out there in the gulf. Lord knows why I lived." He shrugged. "Well, anyway, I was heading for Shuruun when I crashed, and I got here. So why complain?"

He drank again, deeply, and Stark shook his head.

"You've been here nine years, then, by Earth time," he said. He had never met Larrabee, but he remembered the pictures of him that had flashed across space on police bands. Larrabee had been a young man then, dark and proud and handsome.

Larrabee guessed his thought. "I've changed, haven't I?"

Stark said lamely, "Everybody thought you were dead."

Larrabee laughed. After that, for a moment, there was silence. Stark's ears were straining for any sound outside. There was none.

He said abruptly, "What about this trap I'm in?"

"I'll tell you one thing about it," said Larrabee. "There's no way out. I can't help you. I wouldn't if I could, get that straight. But I can't, anyway."

"Thanks," Stark said sourly. "You can at least tell me what goes on."

"Listen," said Larrabee. "I'm a cripple, and an old man, and Shuruun isn't the sweetest place in the solar system to live. But I do live. I have a wife, a slatternly wench I'll admit, but good enough in her way. You'll notice some little dark-haired brats rolling in the mud. They're mine, too. I have some skill at setting bones and such, and so I can get drunk for nothing as often as I will—which is often. Also, because of this bum leg, I'm perfectly safe. So don't ask me what goes on. I take great pains not to know."

Stark said, "Who are the Lhari?"

"Would you like to meet them?" Larrabee seemed to find something very amusing in that thought. "Just go on up to the castle. They live there. They're the Lords of Shuruun, and they're always glad to meet strangers."

He leaned forward suddenly. "Who are you anyway? What's your name, and why the devil did you come here?"

"My name is Stark. And I came here for the same reason you did."

"Stark," repeated Larrabee slowly, his eyes intent. "That rings a faint bell. Seems to me I saw a Wanted flash once, some idiot that had led a native revolt somewhere in the Jovian Colonies—a big cold-eyed brute they referred to colorfully as the wild man from Mercury."

He nodded, pleased with himself. "Wild man, eh? Well, Shuruun will tame you down!"

"Perhaps," said Stark. His eyes shifted constantly, watching Larrabee, watching the doorway and the dark veranda and the people who drank but did not talk among themselves. "Speaking of strangers, one came here at the time of the last rains. He was Venusian, from up coast. A big young man. I used to know him. Perhaps he could help me."

Larrabee snorted. By now, he had drunk his own wine and Stark's too. "Nobody can help you. As for your friend, I never saw him. I'm beginning to think I should never have seen you." Quite suddenly he caught up his stick and got with some difficulty to his feet. He did not look at Stark, but said harshly, "You better get out of here." Then he turned and limped unsteadily to the bar.

Stark rose. He glanced after Larrabee, and again his nostrils twitched to the smell of fear. Then he went out of the tavern the way he had come in, through the front door. No one moved to stop him. Outside, the square was empty. It had begun to rain.

Stark stood for a moment on the steps. He was angry, and filled with a dangerous unease, the hair-trigger nervousness of a tiger that senses the beaters creeping toward him up the wind. He would almost have welcomed the sight of Malthor and the three young men. But there was nothing to fight but the silence and the rain.

He stepped out into the mud, wet and warm around his ankles. An idea came to him, and he smiled, beginning now to move with a definite purpose, along the side of the square.

The sharp downpour strengthened. Rain smoked from Stark's naked shoulders, beat against thatch and mud with a hissing rattle. The harbor had disappeared behind boiling clouds of fog, where water struck the surface of the Red Sea and was turned again instantly by chemical action into vapor. The quays and the neighboring streets were being swallowed up in the impenetrable mist. Lightning came with an eerie bluish flare, and thunder came rolling after it.

Stark turned up the narrow way that led toward the castle.

Its lights were winking out now, one by one, blotted by the creeping fog. Lightning etched its shadowy bulk against the night, and then was gone. And through the noise of the thunder that followed, Stark thought he heard a voice calling.

He stopped, half crouching, his hand on his gun. The cry came again, a girl's voice, thin as the wail of a sea-bird through the driving rain. Then he saw her, a small white blur in the street behind him, running, and even in that dim glimpse of her every line of her body was instinct with fright.

Stark set his back against a wall and waited. There did not seem to be anyone with her, though it was hard to tell in the darkness and the storm.

She came up to him, and stopped, just out of his reach, looking at him and away again with a painful irresoluteness. A bright flash showed her to him clearly. She was young, not long out of her childhood, and pretty in a stupid sort of way. Just now her mouth trembled on the edge of weeping, and her eyes were very large and scared. Her skirt clung to her long thighs, and above it her naked body, hardly fleshed into womanhood, glistened like snow in the wet. Her pale hair hung dripping over her shoulders.

Stark said gently, "What do you want with me?"

She looked at him, so miserably like a wet puppy that he smiled. And as though that smile had taken what little resolution she had out of her, she dropped to her knees, sobbing.

"I can't do it," she wailed. "He'll kill me, but I just can't do it!"

"Do what?" asked Stark.

She stared up at him. "Run away," she urged him. "Rim away now! You'll die in the swamps, but that's better than being one of the Lost Ones!" She shook her thin arms at him. "Run away!"

IV

THE STREET WAS EMPTY. NOTHING SHOWED, NOTHING STIRRED anywhere. Stark leaned over and pulled the girl to her feet, drawing her in under the shelter of the thatched eaves.

"Now then," he said. "Suppose you stop crying and tell me what this is all about."

Presently, between gulps and hiccoughs, he got the story out of her.

"I am Zareth," she said. "Malthor's daughter. He's afraid of you, because of what you did to him on the ship, so he ordered me to watch for you in the square, when you would come out of the tavern. Then I was to follow you, and…"

She broke off, and Stark patted her shoulder. "Go on."

But a new thought had occurred to her. "If I do, will you promise not to beat me, or…" She looked at his gun and shivered.

"I promise."

She studied his face, what she could see of it in the darkness, and then seemed to lose some of her fear.

"I was to stop you. I was to say what I've already said, about being Malthor's daughter and the rest of it, and then I was to say that he wanted me to lead you into an ambush while pretending to help

20

you escape, but that I couldn't do it, and would help you escape any-
how because I hated Malthor and the whole business about the Lost
Ones. So you would believe me, and follow me, and I would lead you
into the ambush."

She shook her head and began to cry again, quietly this time, and
there was nothing of the woman about her at all now. She was just a
child, very miserable and afraid. Stark was glad he had branded Malthor.

"But I can't lead you into the ambush. I do hate Malthor, even
if he is my father, because he beats me. And the Lost Ones..." She
paused. "Sometimes I hear them at night, chanting way out there beyond the mist. It is a very terrible sound."

"It is," said Stark. "I've heard it. Who are the Lost Ones, Zareth?"

"I can't tell you that," said Zareth. "It's forbidden even to speak of
them. And anyway," she finished honestly, "I don't even know. People
disappear, that's all. Not our own people of Shuruun, at least not very
often. But strangers like you—and I'm sure my father goes off into
the swamps to hunt among the tribes there, and I'm sure he comes
back from some of his voyages with nothing in his hold but men from
some captured ship. Why, or what for, I don't know. Except I've heard
the chanting."

"They live out there in the gulf, do they, the Lost Ones?"

"They must. There are many islands there."

"And what of the Lhari, the Lords of Shuruun? Don't they know
what's going on? Or are they part of it?"

She shuddered, and said, "It's not for us to question the Lhari,
nor even to wonder what they do. Those who have are gone from
Shuruun, nobody knows where."

Stark nodded. He was silent for a moment, thinking. Then Zareth's little hand touched his shoulder.

"Go," she said. "Lose yourself in the swamps. You're strong, and
there's something about you different from other men. You may live
to find your way through."

"No. I have something to do before I leave Shuruun." He took Zareth's damp fair head between his hands and kissed her on the forehead. "You're a sweet child, Zareth, and a brave one. Tell Malthor that you did exactly as he told you, and it was not your fault I wouldn't follow you."

"He will beat me anyway," said Zareth philosophically, "but perhaps not quite so hard."

"He'll have no reason to beat you at all, if you tell him the truth—that I would not go with you because my mind was set on going to the castle of the Lhari."

There was a long, long silence, while Zareth's eyes widened slowly in horror, and the rain beat on the thatch, and fog and thunder rolled together across Shuruun.

'To the castle," she whispered. "Oh, no! Go into the swamps, or let Malthor take you—but don't go to the castle!" She took hold of his arm, her fingers biting into his flesh with the urgency of her plea. "You're a stranger, you don't know... Please, don't go up there!"

"Why not?" asked Stark. "Are the Lhari demons? Do they devour men?" He loosened her hands gently. "You'd better go now. Tell your father where I am, if he wishes to come after me."

Zareth backed away slowly, out into the rain, staring at him as though she looked at someone standing on the brink of hell, not dead, but worse than dead. Wonder showed in her face, and through it a great yearning pity. She tried once to speak, and then shook her head and turned away, breaking into a run as though she could not endure to look upon Stark any longer. In a second she was gone.

Stark looked after her for a moment, strangely touched. Then he stepped out into the rain again, heading upward along the steep path that led to the castle of the Lords of Shuruun.

The mist was blinding. Stark had to feel his way, and as he climbed higher, above the level of the town, he was lost in the sullen redness. A hot wind blew, and each flare of lightning turned the crimson fog to a hellish purple. The night was full of a vast hissing where the rain poured into the gulf. He stopped once to hide his gun in a cleft between the rocks.

At length he stumbled against a carven pillar of black stone and found the gate that hung from it, a massive thing sheathed in metal. It was barred, and the pounding of his fists upon it made little sound.

Then he saw the gong, a huge disc of beaten gold beside the gate. Stark picked up the hammer that lay there, and set the deep voice of the gong rolling out between the thunderbolts.

A barred slit opened and a man's eyes looked out at him. Stark dropped the hammer.

"Open up!" he shouted. "I would speak with the Lhari!"

From within he heard an echo of laughter. Scraps of voices came to him on the wind, and then more laughter, and then, slowly, the great valves of the gate creaked open, wide enough only to admit him.

He stepped through, and the gateway shut behind him with a ringing clash.

He stood in a huge open court. Enclosed within its walls was a village of thatched huts, with open sheds for cooking, and behind them were pens for the stabling of beasts, the wingless dragons of the swamps that can be caught and broken to the goad.

He saw this only in vague glimpses, because of the fog. The men who had let him in clustered around him, thrusting him forward into the light that streamed from the huts.

"He would speak with the Lhari!" one of them shouted, to the women and children who stood in the doorways watching. The words were picked up and tossed around the court, and a great burst of laughter went up.

Stark eyed them, saying nothing. They were a puzzling breed. The men, obviously, were soldiers and guards to the Lhari, for they wore the harness of fighting men. As obviously, these were their wives and children, all living behind the castle walls and having little to do with Shuruun.

But it was their racial characteristics that surprised him. They had interbred with the pale tribes of the Swamp-Edges that had peopled

Shuruun, and there were many with milk-white hair and broad faces. Yet even these bore an alien stamp. Stark was puzzled, for the race he would have named was unknown here behind the Mountains of White Cloud, and almost unknown anywhere on Venus at sea level, among the sweltering marshes and the eternal fogs.

They stared at him even more curiously, remarking on his skin and his black hair and the unfamiliar modeling of his face. The women nudged each other and whispered, giggling, and one of them said aloud, "They'll need a barrel-hoop to collar that neck!"

The guards closed in around him. "Well, if you wish to see the Lhari, you shall," said the leader, "but first we must make sure of you."

Spear-points ringed him round. Stark made no resistance while they stripped him of all he had, except for his shorts and sandals. He had expected that, and it amused him, for there was little enough for them to take.

"All right," said the leader. "Come on."

The whole village turned out in the rain to escort Stark to the castle door. There was about them the same ominous interest that the people of Shuruun had had, with one difference. They knew what was supposed to happen to him, knew all about it, and were therefore doubly appreciative of the game.

The great doorway was square and plain, and yet neither crude nor ungraceful. The castle itself was built of the black stone, each block perfectly cut and fitted, and the door itself was sheathed in the same metal as the gate, darkened but not corroded.

The leader of the guard cried out to the warder, "Here is one who would speak with the Lhari!"

The warder laughed. "And so he shall! Their night is long, and dull."

He flung open the heavy door and cried the word down the hallway. Stark could hear it echoing hollowly within, and presently from the shadows came servants clad in silks and wearing jeweled collars, and from the guttural sound of their laughter Stark knew that they had no tongues.

Stark faltered, then. The doorway loomed hollowly before him, and it came to him suddenly that evil lay behind it and that perhaps Zareth was wiser than he when she warned him from the Lhari.

Then he thought of Helvi, and of other things, and lost his fear in anger. Lightning burned the sky. The last cry of the dying storm shook the ground under his feet. He thrust the grinning warder aside and strode into the castle, bringing a veil of the red fog with him, and did not listen to the closing of the door, which was stealthy and quiet as the footfall of approaching Death.

Torches burned here and there along the walls, and by their smoky glare he could see that the hallway was like the entrance—square and unadorned, faced with the black rock. It was high, and wide, and there was about the architecture a calm reflective dignity that had its own beauty, in some ways more impressive than the sensuous loveliness of the ruined palaces he had seen on Mars.

There were no carvings here, no paintings nor frescoes. It seemed that the builders had felt that the hall itself was enough, in its massive perfection of line and the somber gleam of polished stone. The only decoration was in the window embrasures. These were empty now, open to the sky with the red fog wreathing through them, but there were still scraps of jewel-toned panes clinging to the fretwork, to show what they had once been.

A strange feeling swept over Stark. Because of his wild upbringing, he was abnormally sensitive to the sort of impressions that most men receive either dully or not at all.

Walking down the hall, preceded by the tongueless creatures in their bright silks and blazing collars, he was struck by a subtle difference in the place. The castle itself was only an extension of the minds of its builders, a dream shaped into reality. Stark felt that that dark, cool, curiously timeless dream had not originated in a mind like his own, nor like that of any man he had ever seen.

Then the end of the hall was reached, the way barred by low broad doors of gold fashioned in the same chaste simplicity.

A soft scurrying of feet, a shapeless tittering from the servants, a glancing of malicious, mocking eyes. The golden doors swung open, and Stark was in the presence of the Lhari.

V

THEY HAD THE APPEARANCE IN THAT FIRST GLANCE, OF CREATURES glimpsed in a fever-dream, very bright and distant, robed in a misty glow that gave them an illusion of unearthly beauty.

The place in which the Earthman now stood was like a cathedral for breadth and loftiness. Most of it was in darkness, so that it seemed to reach without limit above and on all sides, as though the walls were only shadowy phantasms of the night itself. The polished black stone under his feet held a dim translucent gleam, depthless as water in a black tarn. There was no substance anywhere.

Far away in this shadowy vastness burned a cluster of lamps, a galaxy of little stars to shed a silvery light upon the Lords of Shuruun.

There had been no sound in the place when Stark entered, for the opening of the golden doors had caught the attention of the Lhari and held it in contemplation of the stranger. Stark began to walk toward them in this utter stillness.

Quite suddenly, in the impenetrable gloom somewhere to his right, there came a sharp scuffling and a scratching of reptilian claws, a hissing and a sort of low angry muttering, all magnified and distorted by the echoing vault into a huge demoniac whispering that swept all around him.

Stark whirled around, crouched and ready, his eyes blazing and his body bathed in cold sweat. The noise increased, rushing toward him. From the distant glow of the lamps came a woman's tinkling laughter, thin crystal broken against the vault. The hissing and snarling rose to hollow crescendo, and Stark saw a blurred shape bounding at him.

His hands reached out to receive the rush, but it never came. The strange shape resolved itself into a boy of about ten, who dragged after him on a bit of rope a young dragon, new and toothless from the egg, and protesting with all its strength.

Stark straightened up, feeling let down and furious—and relieved. The boy scowled at him through a forelock of silver curls. Then he called him a very dirty word and rushed away, kicking and hauling at the little beast until it raged like the father of all dragons and sounded like it, too, in that vast echo chamber.

A voice spoke. Slow, harsh, sexless, it rang thinly through the vault. Thin—but a steel blade is thin, too. It speaks inexorably, and its word is final.

The voice said, "Come here, into the light."

Stark obeyed the voice. As he approached the lamps, the aspect of the Lhari changed and steadied. Their beauty remained, but it was not the same. They had looked like angels. Now that he could see them clearly, Stark thought that they might have been the children of Lucifer himself.

There were six of them, counting the boy. Two men, about the same age as Stark, with some complicated gambling game forgotten between them. A woman, beautiful, gowned in white silk, sitting with her hands in her lap, doing nothing. A woman, younger, not so beautiful perhaps, but with a look of stormy and bitter vitality. She wore a short tunic of crimson, and a stout leather glove on her left hand, where perched a flying thing of prey with its fierce eyes hooded. * The boy stood beside the two men, his head poised arrogantly. From time to time he cuffed the little dragon, and it snapped at him with its impotent jaws. He was proud of himself for doing that. Stark wondered how he would behave with the beast when it had grown its fangs.

Opposite him, crouched on a heap of cushions, was a third man. He was deformed, with an ungainly body and long spidery arms, and in his lap a sharp knife lay on a block of wood, half formed into the shape of an obese creature half woman, half pure evil. Stark saw with a flash of surprise that the face of the deformed young man, of all the faces there, was truly human, truly beautiful. His eyes were old in his boyish face, wise, and very sad in their wisdom. He smiled upon the stranger, and his smile was more compassionate than tears.

They looked at Stark, all of them, with restless, hungry eyes. They were the pure breed, that had left its stamp of alienage on the pale-haired folk of the swamps, the serfs who dwelt in the huts outside.

They were of the Cloud People, the folk of the High Plateaus, kings of the land on the farther slopes of the Mountains of White Cloud. It was strange to see them here, on the dark side of the barrier wall, but here they were. How they had come, and why, leaving their rich cool plains for the fetor of these foreign swamps, he could not guess. But there was no mistaking them—the proud fine shaping of their bodies, their alabaster skin, their eyes that were all colors and none, like the dawn sky, their hair that was pure warm silver.

They did not speak. They seemed to be waiting for permission to speak, and Stark wondered which one of them had voiced that steely summons.

Then it came again. "Come here—come closer." And he looked beyond them, beyond the circle of lamps into the shadows again, and saw the speaker.

She lay upon a low bed, her head propped on silken pillows, her vast, her incredibly gigantic body covered with a silken pall. Only her arms were bare, two shapeless masses of white flesh ending in tiny hands. From time to time she stretched one out and took a morsel of food from the supply laid ready beside her, snuffling and wheezing with the effort, and then gulped the tidbit down with a horrible voracity.

Her features had long ago dissolved into a shaking formlessness, with the exception of her nose, which rose out of the fat curved and cruel and thin, like the bony beak of the creature that sat on the girl's wrist and dreamed its hooded dreams of blood. And her eyes...

Stark looked into her eyes and shuddered. Then he glanced at the carving half formed in the cripple's lap, and knew what thought had guided the knife.

Half woman, half pure evil. And strong. Very strong. Her strength lay naked in her eyes for all to see, and it was an ugly strength. It could tear down mountains, but it could never build.

He saw her looking at him. Her eyes bored into his as though they would search out his very guts and study them, and he knew that she expected him to turn away, unable to bear her gaze. He did not. Presently he smiled and said, "I have outstared a rock-lizard, to determine which of us should eat the other. And I've outstared the very rock while waiting for him."

She knew that he spoke the truth. Stark expected her to be angry, but she was not. A vague mountainous rippling shook her and emerged at length as a voiceless laughter.

"You see that?" she demanded, addressing the others. "You whelps of the Lhari—not one of you dares to face me down, yet here is a great dark creature from the gods know where who can stand and shame you."

She glanced again at Stark. "What demon's blood brought you forth, that you have learned neither prudence nor fear?"

Stark answered somberly, "I learned them both before I could walk. But I learned another thing also—a thing called anger."

"And you are angry?"

"Ask Malthor if I am, and why!"

He saw the two men start a little, and a slow smile crossed the girl's face.

"Malthor," said the hulk upon the bed, and ate a mouthful of roast meat dripping with fat. "That is interesting. But rage against Malthor did not bring you here. I am curious, Stranger. Speak."

"I will."

Stark glanced around. The place was a tomb, a trap. The very air smelled of danger. The younger folk watched him in silence. Not one of them had spoken since he came in, except the boy who had cursed him, and that was unnatural in itself. The girl leaned forward, idly stroking the creature on her wrist so that it stirred and ran its knife-like talons in and out of their bony sheaths with sensuous pleasure. Her gaze on Stark was bold and cool, oddly challenging. Of them all, she alone saw him as a man. To the others he was a problem, a diversion—something less than human.

Stark said, "A man came to Shuruun at the time of the last rains. His name was Helvi, and he was son of a little king by Yarell. He came seeking his brother, who had broken taboo and fled for his life. Helvi came to tell him that the ban was lifted, and he might return. Neither one came back."

The small evil eyes were amused, blinking in their tallowy creases. "And so?"

"And so I have come after Helvi, who is my friend."

Again there was the heaving of that bulk of flesh, the explosion of laughter that hissed and wheezed in snakelike echoes through the vault.

"Friendship must run deep with you, Stranger. Ah, well. The Lhari are kind of heart. You shall find your friend."

And as though that were the signal to end their deferential silence, the younger folk burst into laughter also, until the vast hall rang with it, giving back a sound like demons laughing on the edge of Hell.

The cripple only did not laugh, but bent his bright head over his carving, and sighed.

The girl sprang up. "Not yet, Grandmother! Keep him awhile."

The cold, cruel eyes shifted to her. "And what will you do with him, Varra? Haul him about on a string, like Bor with his wretched beast?"

"Perhaps—though I think it would need a stout chain to hold him." Varra turned and looked at Stark, bold and bright, taking in the breadth and the height of him, the shaping of the great smooth muscles, the iron line of the jaw. She smiled. Her mouth was very lovely, like the red fruit of the swamp tree that bears death in its pungent sweetness.

"Here is a man," she said. "The first man I have seen since my father died."

The two men at the gaming table rose, their faces flushed and angry. One of them strode forward and gripped the girl's arm roughly.

"So I am not a man," he said, with surprising gentleness. "A sad thing, for one who is to be your husband. It's best that we settle that now, before we wed."

Varra nodded. Stark saw that the man's fingers were cutting savagely into the firm muscle of her arm, but she did not wince.

"High time to settle it all, Egil. You have borne enough from me. The day is long overdue for my taming. I must learn now to bend my neck, and acknowledge my lord."

For a moment Stark thought she meant it, the note of mockery in her voice was so subtle. Then the woman in white, who all this time had not moved nor changed expression, voiced again the thin, tinkling laugh he had heard once before. From that, and the dark suffusion of blood in Egil's face, Stark knew that Varra was only casting the man's own phrases back at him. The boy let out one derisive bark, and was cuffed into silence.

Varra looked straight at Stark. "Will you fight for me?" she demanded.

Quite suddenly, it was Stark's turn to laugh. "No!" he said.

Varra shrugged. "Very well, then. I must fight for myself."

"Man," snarled Egil. "I'll show you who's a man, you scapegrace little vixen!"

He wrenched off his girdle with his free hand, at the same time bending the girl around so he could get a fair shot at her. The creature of prey clung to her wrist, beating its wings and screaming, its hooded head jerking.

With a motion so quick that it was hardly visible, Varra slipped the hood and flew the creature straight for Egil's face.

He let go, flinging up his arms to ward off the talons and the tearing beak. The wide wings beat and hammered. Egil yelled. The boy Bor got out of range and danced up and down shrieking with delight.

Varra stood quietly. The bruises were blackening on her arm, but she did not deign to touch them. Egil blundered against the gaming table and sent the ivory pieces flying. Then he tripped over a cushion and fell flat, and the hungry talons ripped his tunic to ribbons down the back.

Varra whistled, a clear peremptory call. The creature gave a last peck at the back of Egil's head and flopped sullenly back to its perch on her wrist. She held it, turning toward Stark. He knew from the poise of her that she was on the verge of launching her pet at him. But she studied him and then shook her head.

"No," she said, and slipped the hood back on. "You would kill it."

Egil had scrambled up and gone off into the darkness, sucking a cut on his arm. His face was black with rage. The other man looked at Varra.

"If you were pledged to me," he said, "I'd have that temper out of you!"

"Come and try it," answered Varra.

The man shrugged and sat down. "It's not my place. I keep the peace in my own house." He glanced at the woman in white, and Stark saw that her face, hitherto blank of any expression, had taken on a look of abject fear.

"You do," said Varra, "and, if I were Arel, I would stab you while you slept. But you're safe. She had no spirit to begin with."

Arel shivered and looked steadfastly at her hands. The man began to gather up the scattered pieces. He said casually, "Egil will wring your neck some day, Varra, and I shan't weep to see it."

All this time the old woman had eaten and watched, watched and eaten, her eyes glittering with interest.

"A pretty brood, are they not?" she demanded of Stark. "Full of spirit, quarreling like young hawks in the nest. That's why I keep them around me, so—they are such sport to watch. All except Treon there."

She indicated the crippled youth. "He does nothing. Dull and soft-mouthed, worse than Arel. What a grandson to be cursed with! But his sister has fire enough for two." She munched a sweet, grunting with pride.

Treon raised his head and spoke, and his voice was like music, echoing with an eerie loveliness in that dark place.

"Dull I may be, Grandmother, and weak in body, and without hope. Yet I shall be the last of the Lhari. Death sits waiting on the towers, and he shall gather you all before me. I know, for the winds have told me."

He turned his suffering eyes upon Stark and smiled, a smile of such woe and resignation that the Earthman's heart ached with it. Yet there was a thankfulness in it too, as though some long waiting was over at last.

"You," he said softly, "Stranger with the fierce eyes. I saw you come, out of the darkness, and where you set foot there was a bloody print. Your arms were red to the elbows, and your breast was splashed with the redness, and on your brow was the symbol of death. Then I knew, and the wind whispered into my ear, 'It is so. This man shall pull the castle down, and its stones shall crush Shuruun and set the Lost Ones free.' "

He laughed, very quietly. "Look at him, all of you. For he will be your doom!"

There was a moment's silence, and Stark, with all the superstitions of a wild race thick within him, turned cold to the roots of his hair. Then the old woman said disgustedly, "Have the winds warned you of this, my idiot?"

And with astonishing force and accuracy she picked up a ripe fruit and flung it at Treon.

"Stop your mouth with that," she told him. "I am weary to death of your prophecies."

Treon looked at the crimson juice trickling slowly down the breast of his tunic, to drip upon the carving in his lap. The half formed head was covered with it. Treon was shaken with silent mirth.

"Well," said Varra, coming up to Stark, "what do you think of the Lhari? The proud Lhari, who would not stoop to mingle their blood with the cattle of the swamps. My half-witted brother, my worthless cousins, that little monster Bor who is the last twig of the tree—do you wonder I flew my falcon at Egil?"

She waited for an answer, her head thrown back, the silver curls framing her face like wisps of storm-cloud. There was a swagger about her that at once irritated and delighted Stark. A hellcat, he thought, but a mighty fetching one, and bold as brass. Bold—and honest. Her lips were parted, midway between anger and a smile.

He caught her to him suddenly and kissed her, holding her slim strong body as though she were a doll. He was in no hurry to set her down. When at last he did, he grinned and said, "Was that what you wanted?"

"Yes," answered Varra. "That was what I wanted." She spun about, her jaw set dangerously. "Grandmother…"

She got no farther. Stark saw that the old woman was attempting to sit upright, her face purpling with effort and the most terrible wrath he had ever seen.

"You," she gasped at the girl. She choked on her fury and her shortness of breath, and then Egil came soft-footed into the light, bearing in his hand a thing made of black metal and oddly shaped, with a blunt, thick muzzle.

"Lie back, Grandmother," he said. "I had a mind to use this on Varra—"

Even as he spoke he pressed a stud, and Stark in the act of leaping for the sheltering darkness, crashed down and lay like a dead man. There had been no sound, no flash, nothing, but a vast hand that smote him suddenly into oblivion.

Egil finished,—"but I see a better target."

VI

RED. RED. RED. THE COLOR OF BLOOD. BLOOD IN HIS EYES. He was remembering now. The quarry had turned on him, and they had fought on the bare, blistering rocks.

Nor had N'Chaka killed. The Lord of the Rocks was very big, a giant among lizards, and N'Chaka was small. The Lord of the Rocks had laid open N'Chaka's head before the wooden spear had more than scratched his flank.

It was strange that N'Chaka still lived. The Lord of the Rocks must have been full fed. Only that had saved him.

N'Chaka groaned, not with pain, but with shame. He had failed. Hoping for a great triumph, he had disobeyed the tribal law that forbids a boy to hunt the quarry of a man, and he had failed. Old One would not reward him with the girdle and the flint spear of manhood. Old One would give him to the women for the punishment of little whips. Tika would laugh at him, and it would be many seasons before Old One would grant him permission to try the Man's Hunt.

Blood in his eyes.

He blinked to clear them. The instinct of survival was prodding him. He must arouse himself and creep away, before the Lord of the Rocks returned to eat him.

The redness would not go away. It swam and flowed, strangely sparkling. He blinked again, and tried to lift his head, and could not, and fear struck down upon him like the iron frost of night upon the rocks of the valley.

It was all wrong. He could see himself clearly, a naked boy dizzy with pain, rising and clambering over the ledges and the shale to the safety of the cave. He could see that, and yet he could not move.

All wrong. Time, space, the universe, darkened and turned.

A voice spoke to him. A girl's voice. Not Tika's and the speech was strange.

Tika was dead. Memories rushed through his mind, the bitter things, the cruel things. Old One was dead, and all the others...

The voice spoke again, calling him by a name that was not his own.

Stark.

Memory shattered into a kaleidoscope of broken pictures, fragments, rushing, spinning. He was adrift among them. He was lost, and the terror of it brought a scream into his throat.

Soft hands touching his face, gentle words, swift and soothing. The redness cleared and steadied, though it did not go away, and quite suddenly he was himself again, with all his memories where they belonged.

He was lying on his back, and Zareth, Malthor's daughter, was looking down at him. He knew now what the redness was. He had seen it too often before not to know. He was somewhere at the bottom of the Red Sea—that weird ocean in which a man can breathe.

And he could not move. That had not changed, nor gone away. His body was dead.

The terror he had felt before was nothing, to the agony that filled him now. He lay entombed in his own flesh, staring up at Zareth, wanting an answer to a question he dared not ask.

She understood, from the look in his eyes.

"It's all right," she said, and smiled. "It will wear off. You'll be all right. It's only the weapon of the Lhari. Somehow it puts the body to sleep, but it will wake again."

Stark remembered the black object that Egil had held in his hands. A projector of some sort, then, beaming a current of high-frequency vibration that paralyzed the nerve centers. He was amazed. The Cloud People were barbarians themselves, though on a higher scale than the swamp-edge tribes, and certainly had no such scientific proficiency. He wondered where the Lhari had got hold of such a weapon.

It didn't really matter. Not just now. Relief swept over him, bringing him dangerously close to tears. The effect would wear off. At the moment, that was all he cared about.

He looked up at Zareth again. Her pale hair floated with the slow breathing of the sea, a milky cloud against the spark-shot crimson. He saw now that her face was drawn and shadowed, and there was a terrible hopelessness in her eyes. She had been alive when he first saw her—frightened, not too bright, but full of emotion and a certain dogged courage. Now the spark was gone, crushed out.

She wore a collar around her white neck, a ring of dark metal with the ends fused together for all time.

"Where are we?" he asked.

And she answered, her voice carrying deep and hollow in the dense substance of the sea, "We are in the place of the Lost Ones."

Stark looked beyond her, as far as he could see, since he was unable to turn his head. And wonder came to him.

Black walls, black vault above him, a vast hall filled with the wash of the sea that slipped in streaks of whispering flame through the high embrasures. A hall that was twin to the vault of shadows where he had met the Lhari.

"There is a city," said Zareth dully. "You will see it soon. You will see nothing else until you die."

Stark said, very gently, "How do you come here, little one?"

"Because of my father. I will tell you all I know, which is little enough. Malthor has been slaver to the Lhari for a long time. There are a number of them among the captains of Shuruun, but that is a thing that is never spoken of—so I, his daughter, could only guess. I was sure of it when he sent me after you."

She laughed, a bitter sound. "Now I'm here, with the collar of the Lost Ones on my neck. But Malthor is here, too." She laughed again, ugly laughter to come from a young mouth. Then she looked at Stark, and her hand reached out timidly to touch his hair in what was almost a caress. Her eyes were wide, and soft, and full of tears.

"Why didn't you go into the swamps when I warned you?"

Stark answered stolidly, "Too late to worry about that now." Then, "You say Malthor is here, a slave?"

"Yes." Again, that look of wonder and admiration in her eyes. "I don't know what you said or did to the Lhari, but the Lord Egil came down in a black rage and cursed my father for a bungling fool because he could not hold you. My father whined and made excuses, and all would have been well—only his curiosity got the better of him and he asked the Lord Egil what had happened. You were like a wild beast, Malthor said, and he hoped you had not harmed the Lady Varra, as he could see from Egil's wounds that there had been trouble.

"The Lord Egil turned quite purple. I thought he was going to fall in a fit."

"Yes," said Stark. "That was the wrong thing to say." The ludicrous side of it struck him, and he was suddenly roaring with laughter. "Malthor should have kept his mouth shut!"

"Egil called his guard and ordered them to take Malthor. And when he realized what had happened, Malthor turned on me, trying to say that it was all my fault, that I let you escape."

Stark stopped laughing.

Her voice went on slowly, "Egil seemed quite mad with fury. I have heard that the Lhari are all mad, and I think it is so. At any rate, he ordered me taken too, for he wanted to stamp Malthor's seed into the mud forever. So we are here."

There was a long silence. Stark could think of no word of comfort, and as for hope, he had better wait until he was sure he could at least raise his head. Egil might have damaged him permanently, out of spite. In fact, he was surprised he wasn't dead.

He glanced again at the collar on Zareth's neck. Slave. Slave to the Lhari, in the city of the Lost Ones.

What the devil did they do with slaves, at the bottom of the sea?

The heavy gases conducted sound remarkably well, except for an odd property of diffusion which made it seem that a voice came from everywhere at once. Now, all at once, Stark became aware of a dull clamor of voices drifting towards him.

He tried to see, and Zareth turned his head carefully so that he might.

The Lost Ones were returning from whatever work it was they did.

Out of the dim red murk beyond the open door they swam, into the long, long vastness of the hall that was filled with the same red murk, moving slowly, their white bodies trailing wakes of sullen flame. The host of the damned drifting through a strange red-litten hell, weary and without hope.

One by one they sank onto pallets laid in rows on the black stone floor, and lay there, utterly exhausted, their pale hair lifting and floating with the slow eddies of the sea. And each one wore a collar.

One man did not lie down. He came toward Stark, a tall barbarian who drew himself with great strokes of his arms so that he was wrapped in wheeling sparks. Stark knew his face.

"Helvi," he said, and smiled in welcome.

"Brother!"

Helvi crouched down—a great handsome boy he had been the last time Stark saw him, but he was a man now, with all the laughter turned to grim deep lines around his mouth and the bones of his face standing out like granite ridges.

"Brother," he said again, looking at Stark through a glitter of unashamed tears. "Fool." And he cursed Stark savagely because he had come to Shuruun to look for an idiot who had gone the same way, and was already as good as dead.

"Would you have followed me?" asked Stark.

"But I am only an ignorant child of the swamps," said Helvi. "You come from space, you know the other worlds, you can read and write—you should have better sense!"

Stark grinned. "And I'm still an ignorant child of the rocks. So we're two fools together. Where is Tobal?"

Tobal was Helvi's brother, who had broken taboo and looked for refuge in Shuruun. Apparently he had found peace at last, for Helvi shook his head.

"A man cannot live too long under the sea. It is not enough merely to breathe and eat. Tobal overran his time, and I am close to the end of mine." He held up his hand and then swept it down sharply, watching the broken fires dance along his arms.

"The mind breaks before the body," said Helvi casually, as though it were a matter of no importance.

Zareth spoke. "Helvi has guarded you each period while the others slept."

"And not I alone," said Helvi. "The little one stood with me."

"Guarded me!" said Stark. "Why?"

For answer, Helvi gestured toward a pallet not far away. Malthor lay there, his eyes half open and full of malice, the fresh scar livid on his cheek.

"He feels," said Helvi, "that you should not have fought upon his ship."

Stark felt an inward chill of horror. To lie here helpless, watching Malthor come toward him with open fingers reaching for his helpless throat…

He made a passionate effort to move, and gave up, gasping. Helvi grinned.

"Now is the time I should wrestle you, Stark, for I never could throw you before." He gave Stark's head a shake, very gentle for all its apparent roughness. "You'll be throwing me again. Sleep now, and don't worry."

He settled himself to watch, and presently in spite of himself Stark slept, with Zareth curled at his feet like a little dog.

There was no time down there in the heart of the Red Sea. No daylight, no dawn, no space of darkness. No winds blew, no rain nor storm broke the endless silence. Only the lazy currents whispered by on their way to nowhere, and the red sparks, danced, and the great hall waited, remembering the past.

Stark waited, too. How long he never knew, but he was used to waiting. He had learned his patience on the knees of the great mountains whose heads lift proudly into open space to look at the Sun, and he had absorbed their own contempt for time.

Little by little, life returned to his body. A mongrel guard came now and again to examine him, pricking Stark's flesh with his knife to test the reaction, so that Stark should not malinger.

He reckoned without Stark's control. The Earthman bore his prodding without so much as a twitch until his limbs were completely his own again. Then he sprang up and pitched the man half the length of the hall, turning over and over, yelling with startled anger.

At the next period of labor, Stark was driven with the rest out into the City of the Lost Ones.

VII

Stark had been in places before that oppressed him with a sense of their strangeness or their wickedness—Sinharat, the lovely ruin of coral and gold lost in the Martin wastes; Jekkara, Valkis—the Low-Canal towns that smell of blood and wine; the cliff-caves of Ari-anrhod on the edge of Darkside, the buried tomb-cities of Callisto. But this—this was nightmare to haunt a man's dreams.

He stared about him as he went in the long line of slaves, and felt such a cold shuddering contraction of his belly as he had never known before.

Wide avenues paved with polished blocks of stone, perfect as ebon mirrors. Buildings, tall and stately, pure and plain, with a calm strength that could outlast the ages. Black, all black, with no fripperies of paint or carving to soften them, only here and there a window like a drowned jewel glinting through the red.

Vines like drifts of snow cascading down the stones. Gardens with close-clipped turf and flowers lifting bright on their green stalks, their petals open to a daylight that was gone, their heads bending as though to some forgotten breeze. All neat, all tended, the branches pruned, the fresh soil turned this morning—by whose hand?

Stark remembered the great forest dreaming at the bottom of the gulf, and shivered. He did not like to think how long ago these flowers must have opened their young bloom to the last light they were ever going to see. For they were dead—dead as the forest, dead as the city. Forever bright—and dead.

Stark thought that it must always have been a silent city. It was impossible to imagine noisy throngs flocking to a market square down those immense avenues. The black walls were not made to echo song or laughter. Even the children must have moved quietly along the garden paths, small wise creatures born to an ancient dignity.

He was beginning to understand now the meaning of that weird forest. The Gulf of Shuruun had not always been a gulf. It had been a valley, rich, fertile, with this great city in its arms, and here and there on the upper slopes the retreat of some noble or philosopher—of which the castle of the Lhari was a survivor.

A wall of rock had held back the Red Sea from his valley. And then, somehow, the wall had cracked, and the sullen crimson tide had flowed slowly, slowly into the fertile bottoms, rising higher, lapping the towers and the tree tops in swirling flame, drowning the land forever. Stark wondered if the people had known the disaster was coming, if they had gone forth to tend their gardens for the last time so that they might remain perfect in the embalming gases of the sea.

The columns of slaves, herded by overseers armed with small black weapons similar to the one Egil had used, came out into a broad square whose farther edges were veiled in the red murk. And Stark looked on ruin.

A great building had fallen in the center of the square. The gods only knew what force had burst its walls and tossed the giant blocks like pebbles into a heap. But there it was, the one untidy thing in the city, a mountain of debris.

Nothing else was damaged. It seemed that this had been the place of temples, and they stood unharmed, ranked around the sides of the square, the dim fires rippling through their open porticoes. Deep in their inner shadows Stark thought he could make out images, gigantic things brooding in the spark-shot gloom.

He had no chance to study them. The overseers cursed them on, and now he saw what use the slaves were put to. They were clearing away the wreckage of the fallen building.

Helvi whispered, "For sixteen years men have slaved and died down here, and the work is not half done. And why do the Lhari want it done at all? I'll tell you why. Because they are mad, mad as swamp-dragons gone musth in the spring!"

It seemed madness indeed, to labor at this pile of rocks in a dead city at the bottom of the sea. It was madness. And yet the Lhari, though they might be insane, were not fools. There was a reason for it, and Stark was sure it was a good reason—good for the Lhari, at any rate.

An overseer came up to Stark, thrusting him roughly toward a sledge already partly loaded with broken rocks. Stark hesitated, his eyes turning ugly, and Helvi said,

"Come on, you fool! Do you want to be down flat on your back again?"

Stark glanced at the little weapon, blunt and ready, and turned reluctantly to obey. And there began his servitude.

It was a weird sort of life he led. For a while he tried to reckon time by the periods of work and sleep, but he lost count, and it did not greatly matter anyway.

He labored with the others, hauling the huge blocks away, clearing out the cellars that were partly bared, shoring up weak walls underground. The slaves clung to their old habit of thought, calling the work-periods "days" and the sleep-periods "nights."

Each "day" Egil, or his brother Cond, came to see what had been done, and went away black-browed and disappointed, ordering the work speeded up.

Treon was there also much of the time. He would come slowly in his awkward crabwise way and perch like a pale gargoyle on the stones, never speaking, watching with his sad beautiful eyes. He woke a vague foreboding in Stark. There was something awesome in Treon's silent patience, as though he waited the coming of some black doom, long delayed but inevitable. Stark would remember the prophecy, and shiver.

It was obvious to Stark after a while that the Lhari were clearing the building to get at the cellars underneath. The great dark caverns already bared had yielded nothing, but the brothers still hoped. Over and over Cond and Egil sounded the walls and the floors, prying here and there, and chafing at the delay in opening up the underground labyrinth. What they hoped to find, no one knew.

Varra came, too. Alone, and often, she would drift down through the dim mist-fires and watch, smiling a secret smile, her hair like blown silver where the currents played with it. She had nothing but curt words for Egil, but she kept her eyes on the great dark Earthman, and there was a look in them that stirred his blood. Egil was not blind, and it stirred his too, but in a different way.

Zareth saw that look. She kept as close to Stark as possible, asking no favors, but following him around with a sort of quiet devotion, seeming contented only when she was near him. One "night" in the slave barracks she crouched beside his pallet, her hand on his bare knee. She did not speak, and her face was hidden by the floating masses of her hair.

Stark turned her head so that he could see her, pushing the pale cloud gently away.

"What troubles you, little sister?"

Her eyes were wide and shadowed with some vague fear. But she only said, "It's not my place to speak."

"Why not?"

"Because..." Her mouth trembled, and then suddenly she said, "Oh, it's foolish, I know. But the woman of the Lhari..."

"What about her?"

"She watches you. Always she watches you! And the Lord Egil is angry. There is something in her mind, and it will bring you only evil. I know it!"

"It seems to me," said Stark wryly, "that the Lhari have already done as much evil as possible to all of us."

"No," answered Zareth, with an odd wisdom. "Our hearts are still clean."

Stark smiled. He leaned over and kissed her. "I'll be careful, little sister."

Quite suddenly she flung her arms around his neck and clung to him tightly, and Stark's face sobered. He patted her, rather awkwardly, and then she had gone, to curl up on her own pallet with her head buried in her arms.

Stark lay down. His heart was sad, and there was a stinging moisture in his eyes.

The red eternities dragged on. Stark learned what Helvi had meant when he said that the mind broke before the body. The sea bottom was no place for creatures of the upper air. He learned also the meaning of the metal collars, and the manner of Tobal's death.

Helvi explained.

"There are boundaries laid down. Within them we may range, if we have the strength and the desire after work. Beyond them we may not go. And there is no chance of escape by breaking through the barrier. How this is done I do not understand, but it is so, and the collars are the key to it.

"When a slave approaches the barrier the collar brightens as though with fire, and the slave falls. I have tried this myself, and I know. Half paralyzed, you may still crawl back to safety. But if you are mad, as Tobal was, and charge the barrier strongly…"

He made a cutting motion with his hands.

Stark nodded. He did not attempt to explain electricity or electronic vibrations to Helvi, but it seemed plain enough that the force with which the Lhari kept their slaves in check was something of the sort. The collars acted as conductors, perhaps for the same type of beam that was generated in the hand-weapons. When the metal broke the invisible boundary line it triggered off a force-beam from the central power station, in the manner of the obedient electric eye that opens doors and rings alarm bells. First a warning—then death.

The boundaries were wide enough, extending around the city and enclosing a good bit of forest beyond it. There was no possibility of a slave hiding among the trees, because the collar could be traced by the same type of beam, turned to low power, and the punishment meted out to a retaken man was such that few were foolish enough to try that game.

The surface, of course, was utterly forbidden. The one unguarded spot was the island where the central power station was, and here the slaves were allowed to come sometimes at night. The Lhari had discovered that they lived longer and worked better if they had an occasional breath of air and a look at the sky.

Many times Stark made that pilgrimage with the others. Up from the red depths they would come, through the reeling bands of fire where the currents ran, through the clouds of crimson sparks and the sullen patches of stillness that were like pools of blood, a company of white ghosts shrouded in flame, rising from their tomb for a little taste of the world they had lost.

It didn't matter that they were so weary they had barely the strength to get back to the barracks and sleep. They found the strength. To walk again on the open ground, to be rid of the eternal crimson dusk and the oppressive weight on the chest—to look up into the hot blue night of Venus and smell the fragrance of the liha-trees borne on the land wind…They found the strength.

They sang here, sitting on the island rocks and staring through the mists toward the shore they would never see again. It was their chanting that Stark had heard when he came down the gulf with Malthor, that wordless cry of grief and loss. Now he was here himself, holding Zareth close to comfort her and joining his own deep voice into that primitive reproach to the gods.

While he sat, howling like the savage he was, he studied the power plant, a squat blockhouse of a place. On the nights the slaves came guards were stationed outside to warn them away. The blockhouse was doubly guarded with the shock-beam. To attempt to take it by force would only mean death for all concerned.

Stark gave that idea up for the time being. There was never a second when escape was not in his thoughts, but he was too old in the game to break his neck against a stone wall. Like Malthor, he would wait.

Zareth and Helvi both changed after Stark's coming. Though they never talked of breaking free, both of them lost their air of hopelessness. Stark made neither plans nor promises. But Helvi knew him from of old, and the girl had her own subtle understanding, and they held up their heads again.

Then, one "day" as the work was ending, Varra came smiling out of the red murk and beckoned to him, and Stark's heart gave a great leap. Without a backward look he left Helvi and Zareth, and went with her, down the wide still avenue that led outward to the forest.

VIII

THEY LEFT THE STATELY BUILDINGS AND THE WIDE SPACES BEHIND them, and went in among the trees. Stark hated the forest. The city was bad enough, but it was dead, honestly dead, except for those neat nightmare gardens. There was something terrifying about these great trees, full-leafed and green, rioting with flowering vines and all the rich undergrowth of the jungle, standing like massed corpses made lovely by mortuary art They swayed and rustled as the coiling fires swept them, branches bending to that silent horrible parody of wind. Stark always felt trapped there, and stifled by the stiff leaves and the vines.

But he went, and Varra slipped like a silver bird between the great trunks, apparently happy.

"I have come here often, ever since I was old enough. It's wonderful. Here I can stoop and fly like one of my own hawks." She laughed and plucked a golden flower to set in her hair, and then darted away again, her white legs flashing.

Stark followed. He could see what she meant. Here in this strange sea one's motion was as much flying as swimming, since the pressure equalized the weight of the body. There was a queer sort of thrill in plunging headlong from the tree tops, to arrow down through a tangle of vines and branches and then sweep upward again.

She was playing with him, and he knew it. The challenge got his blood up. He could have caught her easily but he did not, only now and again he circled her to show his strength. They sped on and on, trailing wakes of flame, a black hawk chasing a silver dove through the forests of a dream.

But the dove had been fledged in an eagle's nest. Stark wearied of the game at last. He caught her and they clung together, drifting still among the trees with the momentum of that wonderful weightless flight.

Her kiss at first was lazy, teasing and curious. Then it changed. All Stark's smoldering anger leaped into a different kind of flame. His handling of her was rough and cruel, and she laughed, a little fierce voiceless laugh, and gave it back to him, and he remembered how he had thought her mouth was like a bitter fruit that would give a man pain when he kissed it.

She broke away at last and came to rest on a broad branch, leaning back against the trunk and laughing, her eyes brilliant and cruel as Stark's own. And Stark sat down at her feet.

"What do you want?" he demanded. "What do you want with me?"

She smiled. There was nothing sidelong or shy about her. She was bold as a new blade.

"I'll tell you, wild man."

He started. "Where did you pick up that name?"

"I have been asking the Earthman Larrabee about you. It suits you well." She leaned forward. "This is what I want of you. Slay me Egil and his brother Cond. Also Bor, who will grow up worse than either—although that I can do myself, if you're averse to killing children, though Bor is more monster than child. Grandmother can't live forever, and with my cousins out of the way she's no threat. Treon doesn't count."

"And if I do—what then?"

"Freedom. And me. You'll rule Shuruun at my side."

Stark's eyes were mocking. "For how long, Varra?"

"Who knows? And what does it matter? The years take care of themselves." She shrugged. "The Lhari blood has run out, and it's time there was a fresh strain. Our children will rule after us, and they'll be men."

Stark laughed. He roared with it.

"It's not enough that I'm a slave to the Lhari. Now I must be executioner and herd bull as well!" He looked at her keenly. "Why me, Varra? Why pick on me?"

"Because, as I have said, you are the first man I have seen since my father died. Also, there is something about you..."

She pushed herself upward to hover lazily, her lips just brushing his.

"Do you think it would be so bad a thing to live with me, wild man?"

She was lovely and maddening, a silver witch shining among the dim fires of the sea, full of wickedness and laughter. Stark reached out and drew her to him.

"Not bad," he murmured. "Dangerous."

He kissed her, and she whispered, "I think you're not afraid of danger,"

"On the contrary, I'm a cautious man." He held her off, where he could look straight into her eyes. "I owe Egil something on my own, but I will not murder. The fight must be fair, and Cond will have to take care of himself."

"Fair! Was Egil fair with you—or me?"

He shrugged. "My way, or not at all."

She thought it over a while, then nodded. "All right. As for Cond, you will give him a blood debt, and pride will make him fight. The Lhari are all proud," she added bitterly. "That's our curse. But it's bred in the bone, as you'll find out."

"One more thing. Zareth and Helvi are to go free, and there must be an end to this slavery."

She stared at him. "You drive a hard bargain, wild man!"

"Yes or no?"

"Yes or no?"

"Yes and no. Zareth and Helvi you may have, if you insist, though the gods know what you see in that pallid child. As to the other..." She smiled very mockingly. "I'm no fool, Stark. You're evading me, and two can play that game."

He laughed. "Fair enough. And now tell me this, witch with the silver curls—how am I to get at Egil that I may kill him?"

"I'll arrange that."

She said it with such vicious assurance that he was pretty sure she would arrange it. He was silent for a moment, and then he asked,

"Varra—what are the Lhari searching for at the bottom of the sea?"

She answered slowly, "I told you that we are a proud clan. We were driven out of the High Plateaus centuries ago because of our pride. Now it's all we have left, but it's a driving thing."

She paused, and then went on. "I think we had known about the city for a long time, but it had never meant anything until my father became fascinated by it. He would stay down here days at a time, exploring,, and it was he who found the weapons and the machine of power which is on the island. Then he found the chart and the metal book, hidden away in a secret place. The book was written in pictographs—as though it was meant to be deciphered—and the chart showed the square with the ruined building and the temples, with a separate diagram of catacombs underneath the ground.

"The book told of a secret—a thing of wonder and of fear. And my father believed that the building had been wrecked to close the entrance to the catacombs where the secret was kept. He determined to find it."

Sixteen years of other men's lives. Stark shivered. "What was the secret, Varra?"

"The manner of controlling life. How it was done I do not know, but with it one might build a race of giants, of monsters, or of gods. You can see what that would mean to us, a proud and dying clan."

"Yes," Stark answered slowly. "I can see."

The magnitude of the idea shook him. The builders of the city must have been wise indeed in their scientific research to evolve such a terrible power. To mold the living cells of the body to one's will—to create, not life itself but its form and fashion…

A race of giants, or of gods. The Lhari would like that. To transform their own degenerate flesh into something beyond the race of men, to develop their followers into a corps of fighting men that no one could stand against, to see that their children were given an unholy advantage over all the children of men… Stark was appalled at the realization of the evil they could do if they ever found that secret.

Varra said, "There was a warning in the book. The meaning of it was not quite clear, but it seemed that the ancient ones felt that they had sinned against the gods and been punished, perhaps by some plague. They were a strange race, and not human. At any rate, they destroyed the great building there as a barrier against anyone who should come after them, and then let the Red Sea in to cover their city forever. They must have been superstitious children, for all their knowledge."

"Then you all ignored the warning, and never worried that a whole city had died to prove it."

She shrugged. "Oh, Treon has been muttering prophecies about it for years. Nobody listens to him. As for myself, I don't care whether we find the secret or not. My belief is it was destroyed along with the building, and besides, I have no faith in such things."

"Besides," mocked Stark shrewdly, "you wouldn't care to see Egil and Cond striding across the heavens of Venus, and you're doubtful just what your own place would be in the new pantheon."

She showed her teeth at him. "You're too wise for your own good. And now goodbye." She gave him a quick, hard kiss and was gone, flashing upward, high above the treetops where he dared not follow.

Stark made his way slowly back to the city, upset and very thoughtful.

As he came back into the great square, heading toward the barracks, he stopped, every nerve taut.

Somewhere, in one of the shadowy temples, the clapper of a votive bell was swinging, sending its deep pulsing note across the silence. Slowly, slowly, like the beating of a dying heart it came, and mingled with it was the faint sound of Zareth's voice, calling his name.

IX

HE CROSSED THE SQUARE, MOVING VERY CAREFULLY THROUGH the red murk, and presently he saw her.

It was not hard to find her. There was one temple larger than all the rest. Stark judged that it must once have faced the entrance of the fallen building, as though the great figure within was set to watch over the scientists and the philosophers who came there to dream their vast and sometimes terrible dreams.

The philosophers were gone, and the scientists had destroyed themselves. But the image still watched over the drowned city, its hand raised both in warning and in benediction.

Now, across its reptilian knees, Zareth lay. The temple was open on all sides, and Stark could see her clearly, a little white scrap of humanity against the black unhuman figure.

Malthor stood beside her. It was he who had been tolling the votive bell. He had stopped now, and Zareth's words came clearly to Stark.

"Go away, go away! They're waiting for you. Don't come in here!"

"I'm waiting for you, Stark," Malthor called out, smiling. "Are you afraid to come?" And he took Zareth by the hair and struck her, slowly and deliberately, twice across the face.

All expression left Stark's face, leaving it perfectly blank except for his eyes, which took on a sudden lambent gleam. He began to move toward the temple, not hurrying even then, but moving in such a way that it seemed an army could not have stopped him.

Zareth broke free from her father. Perhaps she was intended to break free.

"Egil!" she screamed. "It's a trap…"

Again Malthor caught her and this time he struck her harder, so that she crumpled down again across the image that watched with its jeweled, gentle eyes and saw nothing.

"She's afraid for you," said Malthor. "She knows I mean to kill you if I can. Well, perhaps Egil is here also. Perhaps he is not. But certainly Zareth is here. I have beaten her well, and I shall beat her again, as long as she lives to be beaten, for her treachery to me. And if you want to save her from that, you outland dog, you'll have to kill me. Are you afraid?"

Stark was afraid. Malthor and Zareth were alone in the temple. The pillared colonnades were empty except for the dim fires of the sea. Yet Stark was afraid, for an instinct older than speech warned him to be.

It did not matter. Zareth's white skin was mottled with dark bruises, and Malthor was smiling at him, and it did not matter.

Under the shadow of the roof and down the colonnade he went, swiftly now, leaving a streak of fire behind him. Malthor looked into his eyes, and his smile trembled and was gone.

He crouched. And at the last moment, when the dark body plunged down at him as a shark plunges, he drew a hidden knife from his girdle and struck.

Stark had not counted on that. The slaves were searched for possible weapons every day, and even a sliver of stone was forbidden. Somebody must have given it to him, someone…

The thought flashed through his mind while he was in the very act of trying to avoid that death blow. Too late, too late, because his own momentum carried him onto the point…

Reflexes quicker than any man's, the hair-trigger reactions of a wild thing. Muscles straining, the center of balance shifted with an awful wrenching effort, hands grasping at the fire-shot redness as though to force it to defy its own laws. The blade ripped a long shallow gash across his breast. But it did not go home. By a fraction of an inch, it did not go home.

While Stark was still off balance, Malthor sprang.

They grappled. The knife blade glittered redly, a hungry tongue eager to taste Stark's life. The two men rolled over and over, drifting and tumbling erratically, churning the sea to a froth of sparks, and still the image watched, its calm reptilian features unchangingly benign and wise. Threads of a darker red laced heavily across the dancing fires.

Stark got Malthor's arm under his own and held it there with both hands. His back was to the man now. Malthor kicked and clawed with his feet against the backs of Stark's thighs, and his left arm came up and tried to clamp around Stark's throat. Stark buried his chin so that it could not, and then Malthor's hand began to tear at Stark's face, searching for his eyes.

Stark voiced a deep bestial sound in his throat. He moved his head suddenly, catching Malthor's hand between his jaws. He did not let go. Presently his teeth were locked against the thumb-joint, and Malthor was screaming, but Stark could give all his attention to what he was doing with the arm that held the knife. His eyes had changed. They were all beast now, the eyes of a killer blazing cold and beautiful in his dark face.

There was a dull crack, and the arm ceased to strain or fight. It bent back upon itself, and the knife fell, drifting quietly down. Malthor was beyond screaming now. He made one effort to get away as Stark released him, but it was a futile gesture, and he made no sound as Stark broke his neck.

He thrust the body from him. It drifted away, moving lazily with the suck of the currents through the colonnade, now and again touching a black pillar as though in casual wonder, wandering out at last into the square. Malthor was in no hurry. He had all eternity before him.

Stark moved carefully away from the girl, who was trying feebly now to sit up on the knees of the image. He called out, to some unseen presence hidden in the shadows under the roof,

"Malthor screamed your name, Egil. Why didn't you come?"

There was a flicker of movement in the intense darkness of the ledge at the top of the pillars.

"Why should I?" asked the Lord Egil of the Lhari. "I offered him his freedom if he could kill you, but it seems he could not—even though I gave him a knife, and drugs to keep your friend Helvi out of the way."

He came out where Stark could see him, very handsome in a tunic of yellow silk, the blunt black weapon in his hands.

"The important thing was to bait a trap. You would not face me because of this—" He raised the weapon. "I might have killed you as you worked, of course, but my family would have had hard things to say about that. You're a phenomenally good slave."

"They'd have said hard words like 'coward,' Egil," Stark said softly. "And Varra would have set her bird at you in earnest."

Egil nodded. His lip curved cruelly. "Exactly. That amused you, didn't it? And now my little cousin is training another falcon to swoop at me. She hooded you today, didn't she, Outlander?"

He laughed. "Ah well. I didn't kill you openly because there's a better way. Do you think I want it gossiped all over the Red Sea that my cousin jilted me for a foreign slave? Do you think I wish it known that I hated you, and why? No. I would have killed Malthor anyway, if you hadn't done it, because he knew. And when I have killed you and the girl I shall take your bodies to the barrier and leave them there together, and it will be obvious to everyone, even Varra, that you were killed trying to escape."

The weapon's muzzle pointed straight at Stark, and Egil's finger quivered on the trigger stud. Full power, this time. Instead of paralysis, death. Stark measured the distance between himself and Egil. He would be dead before he struck, but the impetus of his leap might carry him on, and give Zareth a chance to escape. The muscles of his thighs stirred and tensed.

A voice said, "And will it be obvious how and why I died, Egil? For if you kill them, you must kill me too."

Where Treon had come from, or when, Stark did not know. But he was there by the image, and his voice was full of a strong music, and his eyes shone with a fey light.

Egil had started, and now he swore in fury. "You idiot! You twisted freak! How did you come here?"

"How does the wind come, and the rain? I am not as other men." He laughed, a somber sound with no mirth in it. "I am here, Egil, and that's all that matters. And you will not slay this stranger who is more beast than man, and more man than any of us. The gods have a use for him."

He had moved as he spoke, until now he stood between Stark and Egil.

"Get out of the way," said Egil.

Treon shook his head.

"Very well," said Egil. "If you wish to die, you may."

The fey gleam brightened in Treon's eyes. "This is a day of death," he said softly, "but not of his, or mine."

Egil said a short, ugly word, and raised the weapon up.

Things happened very quickly after that. Stark sprang, arching up and over Treon's head, cleaving the red gases like a burning arrow. Egil started back, and shifted his aim upward, and his finger snapped down on the trigger stud.

Something white came between Stark and Egil, and took the force of the bolt.

Something white. A girl's body, crowned with streaming hair, and a collar of metal glowing bright around the slender neck.

Zareth.

They had forgotten her, the beaten child crouched on the knees of the image. Stark had moved to keep her out of danger, and she was no threat to the mighty Egil, and Treon's thoughts were known only to himself and the winds that taught him. Unnoticed, she had crept to a place where one last plunge would place her between Stark and death.

The rush of Stark's going took him on over her, except that her hair brushed softly against his skin. Then he was on top of Egil, and it had all been done so swiftly that the Lord of the Lhari had not had time to loose another bolt.

Stark tore the weapon from Egil's hand. He was cold, icy cold, and there was a strange blindness on him, so that he could see nothing clearly but Egil's face. And it was Stark who screamed this time, a dreadful sound like the cry of a great cat gone beyond reason or fear.

Treon stood watching. He watched the blood stream darkly into the sea, and he listened to the silence come, and he saw the thing that had been his cousin drift away on the slow tide, and it was as though he had seen it all before and was not surprised.

Stark went to Zareth's body. The girl was still breathing, very faintly, and her eyes turned to Stark, and she smiled.

Stark was blind now with tears. All his rage had run out of him with Egil's blood, leaving nothing but an aching pity and a sadness, and a wondering awe. He took Zareth very tenderly into his arms and held her, dumbly, watching the tears fall on her upturned face. And presently he knew that she was dead.

Sometime later Treon came to him and said softly, "To this end she was born, and she knew it, and was happy. Even now she smiles. And she should, for she had a better death than most of us." He laid his hand on Stark's shoulder. "Come, I'll show you where to put her. She will be safe there, and tomorrow you can bury her where she would wish to be."

Stark rose and followed him, bearing Zareth in his arms.

Treon went to the pedestal on which the image sat. He pressed in a certain way upon a series of hidden springs, and a section of the paving slid noiselessly back, revealing stone steps leading down.

X

Treon led the way down, into darkness that was lightened only by the dim fires they themselves woke in passing. No currents ran here. The red gas lay dull and stagnant, closed within the walls of a square passage built of the same black stone.

"These are the crypts," he said. "The labyrinth that is shown on the chart my father found." And he told about the chart, as Varra had.

He led the way surely, his misshapen body moving without hesitation past the mouths of branching corridors and the doors of chambers whose interiors were lost in shadow.

"The history of the city is here. All the books and the learning, that they had not the heart to destroy. There are no weapons. They were not a warlike people, and I think that the force we of the Lhari have used differently was defensive only, protection against the beasts and the raiding primitives of the swamps."

With a great effort, Stark wrenched his thoughts away from the light burden he carried.

"I thought," he said dully, "that the crypts were under the wrecked building."

"So we all thought. We were intended to think so. That is why the building was wrecked. And for sixteen years we of the Lhari have killed men and women with dragging the stones of it away. But the temple was shown also in the chart. We thought it was there merely as a landmark, an identification for the great building. But I began to wonder…"

"How long have you known?"

"Not long. Perhaps two rains. It took many seasons to find the secret of this passage. I came here at night, when the others slept."

"And you didn't tell?"

"No!" said Treon. "You are thinking that if I had told, there would have been an end to the slavery and the death. But what then? My family, turned loose with the power to destroy a world, as this city was destroyed? No! It was better for the slaves to die."

He motioned Stark aside, then, between doors of gold that stood ajar, into a vault so great that there was no guessing its size in the red and shrouding gloom.

"This was the burial place of their kings," said Treon softly. "Leave the little one here."

Stark looked around him, still too numb to feel awe, but impressed even so.

They were set in straight lines, the beds of black marble—lines so long that there was no end to them except the limit of vision. And on them slept the old kings, their bodies, marvelously embalmed, covered with silken palls, their hands crossed upon their breasts, their wise unhuman faces stamped with the mark of peace.

Very gently, Stark laid Zareth down on a marble couch, and covered her also with silk, and closed her eyes and folded her hands. And it seemed to him that her face, too, had that look of peace.

He went out with Treon, thinking that none of them had earned a better place in the hall of kings than Zareth.

"Treon," he said.

"Yes?"

"That prophecy you spoke when I came to the castle—I will bear it out."

Treon nodded. "That is the way of prophecies."

He did not return toward the temple, but led the way deeper into the heart of the catacombs. A great excitement burned within him, a bright and terrible thing that communicated itself to Stark. Treon had suddenly taken on the stature of a figure of destiny, and the Earthman had the feeling that he was in the grip of some current that would plunge on irresistibly until everything in its path was swept away. Stark's flesh quivered.

They reached the end of the corridor at last. And there, in the red gloom, a shape sat waiting before a black, barred door. A shape grotesque and incredibly misshapen, so horribly malformed that by it Treon's crippled body appeared almost beautiful. Yet its face was as the faces of the images and the old kings, and its sunken eyes had once held wisdom, and one of its seven-fingered hands was still slim and sensitive.

Stark recoiled. The thing made him physically sick, and he would have turned away, but Treon urged him on.

"Go closer. It is dead, embalmed, but it has a message for you. It has waited all this time to give that message."

Reluctantly, Stark went forward.

Quite suddenly, it seemed that the thing spoke.

Behold me. Look upon me, and take counsel before you grasp that power which lies beyond the door!

Stark leaped back, crying out, and Treon smiled.

"It was so with me. But I have listened to it many times since then. It speaks not with a voice, but within the mind, and only when one has passed a certain spot."

Stark's reasoning mind pondered over that. A thought-record, obviously, triggered off by an electronic beam. The ancients had taken good care that their warning would be heard and understood by anyone who should solve the riddle of the catacombs. Thought-images, speaking directly to the brain, know no barrier of time or language.

He stepped forward again, and once more the telepathic voice spoke to him.

"We tampered with the secrets of the gods. We intended no evil. It was only that we love perfection, and wished to shape all living things as flawless as our buildings and our gardens. We did not know that it was against the Law...

"I was one of those who found the way to change the living cell. We used the unseen force that comes from the Land of the Gods beyond the sky, and we so harnessed it that we could build from the living flesh as the potter builds from the clay. We healed the halt and the maimed, and made those stand tall and straight who came crooked from the egg, and for a time we were as brothers to the gods themselves. I myself, even I, knew the glory of perfection. And then came the reckoning.

"The cell, once made to change, would not stop changing. The growth was slow, and for a while we did not notice it, but when we did it was too late. We were becoming a city of monsters. And the force we had used was worse than useless, for the more we tried to mold the monstrous flesh to its normal shape, the more the stimulated cells grew and grew, until the bodies we labored over were like things of wet mud that flow and change even as you look at them.

"One by one the people of the city destroyed themselves. And those of us who were left realized the judgment of the gods, and our duty. We made all things ready, and let the Red Sea hide us forever from our own kind, and those who should come after.

"Yet we did not destroy our knowledge. Perhaps it was our pride only that forbade us, but we could not bring ourselves to do it. Perhaps other gods, other races wiser than we, can take away the evil and keep only the good. For it is good for all creatures to be, if not perfect, at least strong and sound.

"But heed this warning, whoever you may be that listen. If your gods are jealous, if your people have not the wisdom or the knowledge to succeed where we failed in controlling this force, then touch it not! Or you, and all your people, will become as I."

The voice stopped. Stark moved back again, and said to Treon incredulously, "And your family would ignore that warning?"

Treon laughed. "They are fools. They are cruel and greedy and very proud. They would say that this was a lie to frighten away intruders, or that human flesh would not be subject to the laws that govern the flesh of reptiles. They would say anything, because they have dreamed this dream too long to be denied."

Stark shuddered and looked at the black door. "The thing ought to be destroyed."

"Yes," said Treon softly.

His eyes were shining, looking into some private dream of his own. He started forward, and when Stark would have gone with him he thrust him back, saying, "No. You have no part in this." He shook his head.

"I have waited," he whispered, almost to himself. "The winds bade me wait, until the day was ripe to fall from the tree of death. I have waited, and at dawn I knew, for the wind said, Now is the gathering of the fruit at hand."

He looked suddenly at Stark, and his eyes had in them a clear sanity, for all their feyness.

"You heard, Stark. 'We made those stand tall and straight who came crooked from the egg.' I will have my hour. I will stand as a man for the little time that is left."

He turned, and Stark made no move to follow. He watched Treon's twisted body recede, white against the red dusk, until it passed the monstrous watcher and came to the black door. The long thin arms reached up and pushed the bar away.

The door swung slowly back. Through the opening Stark glimpsed a chamber that held a structure of crystal rods and discs mounted on a frame of metal, the whole thing glowing and glittering with a restless bluish light that dimmed and brightened as though it echoed some vast pulse-beat. There was other apparatus, intricate banks of tubes and condensers, but this was the heart of it, and the heart was still alive.

Treon passed within and closed the door behind him.

Stark drew back some distance from the door and its guardian, crouched down, and set his back against the wall. He thought about the apparatus. Cosmic rays, perhaps—the unseen force that came from beyond the sky. Even yet, all their potentialities were not known. But a few luckless spacemen had found that under certain conditions they could do amazing things to human tissue.

It was a line of thought Stark did not like at all. He tried to keep his mind away from Treon entirely. He tried not to think at all. It was dark there in the corridor, and very still, and the shapeless horror sat quiet in the doorway and waited with him. Stark began to shiver, a shallow animal-twitching of the flesh.

He waited. After a while he thought Treon must be dead, but he did not move. He did not wish to go into that room to see.

He waited.

Suddenly he leaped up, cold sweat bursting out all over him. A crash had echoed down the corridor, a clashing of shattered crystal and a high singing note that trailed off into nothing.

The door opened.

A man came out. A man tall and straight and beautiful as an angel, a strong-limbed man with Treon's face, Treon's tragic eyes. And behind him the chamber was dark. The pulsing heart of power had stopped.

The door was shut and barred again. Treon's voice was saying, "There are records left, and much of the apparatus, so that the secret is not lost entirely. Only it is out of reach."

He came to Stark and held out his hand. "Let us fight together, as men. And do not fear. I shall die, long before this body changes." He smiled, the remembered smile that was full of pity for all living things. "I know, for the winds have told me."

Stark took his hand and held it.

"Good," said Treon. "And now lead on, stranger with the fierce eyes. For the prophecy is yours, and the day is yours, and I who have crept about like a snail all my life know little of battles. Lead, and I will follow."

Stark fingered the collar around his neck. "Can you rid me of this?"

Treon nodded. "There are tools and acid in one of the chambers."

He found them, and worked swiftly, and while he worked Stark thought, smiling—and there was no pity in that smile at all.

They came back at last into the temple, and Treon closed the entrance to the catacombs. It was still night, for the square was empty of slaves. Stark found Egil's weapon where it had fallen, on the ledge where Egil died.

"We must hurry," said Stark. "Come on."

XI

THE ISLAND WAS SHROUDED HEAVILY IN MIST AND THE BLUE darkness of the night. Stark and Treon crept silently among the rocks until they could see the glimmer of torchlight through the window-slits of the power station.

There were seven guards, five inside the blockhouse, two outside to patrol.

When they were close enough, Stark slipped away, going like a shadow, and never a pebble turned under his bare foot. Presently he found a spot to his liking and crouched down. A sentry went by not three feet away, yawning and looking hopefully at the sky for the first signs of dawn.

Treon's voice rang out, the sweet unmistakable voice. "Ho, there, guards!"

The sentry stopped and whirled around. Off around the curve of the stone wall someone began to run, his sandals thud-thudding on the soft ground, and the second guard came up.

"Who speaks?" one demanded. "The Lord Treon?"

They peered into the darkness, and Treon answered, "Yes." He had come forward far enough so that they could make out the pale blur of his face, keeping his body out of sight among the rocks and the shrubs that sprang up between them.

"Make haste," he ordered. "Bid them open the door, there." He spoke in breathless jerks, as though spent. "A tragedy—a disaster! Bid them open!"

One of the men leaped to obey, hammering on the massive door that was kept barred from the inside. The other stood goggle-eyed, watching. Then the door opened, spilling a flood of yellow torchlight into the red fog.

"What is it?" cried the men inside. "What has happened?"

"Come out!" gasped Treon. "My cousin is dead, the Lord Egil is dead, murdered by a slave."

He let that sink in. Three or more men came outside into the circle of light, and their faces were frightened, as though somehow they feared they might be held responsible for this thing.

"You know him," said Treon. "The great black-haired one from Earth. He has slain the Lord Egil and got away into the forest, and we need all extra guards to go after him, since many must be left to guard the other slaves, who are mutinous. You, and you—" He picked out the four biggest ones. "Go at once and join the search. I will stay here with the others."

It nearly worked. The four took a hesitant step or two, and then one paused and said doubtfully,

"But, my lord, it is forbidden that we leave our posts, for any reason. Any reason at all, my lord! The Lord Cond would slay us if we left this place."

"And you fear the Lord Cond more than you do me," said Treon philosophically. "Ah, well. I understand."

He stepped out, full into the light.

A gasp went up, and then a startled yell. The three men from inside had come out armed only with swords, but the two sentries had their shock-weapons. One of them shrieked, "It is a demon, who speaks with Treon's voice!"

And the two black weapons started up.

Behind them, Stark fired two silent bolts in quick succession, and the men fell, safely out of the way for hours. Then he leaped for the door.

He collided with two men who were doing the same thing. The third had turned to hold Treon off with his sword until they were safely inside.

Seeing that Treon, who was unarmed, was in danger of being spitted on the man's point, Stark fired between the two lunging bodies as he fell, and brought the guard down. Then he was involved in a thrashing tangle of arms and legs, and a lucky blow jarred the shock-weapon out of his hand.

Treon added himself to the fray. Pleasuring in his new strength, he caught one man by the neck and pulled him off. The guards were big men, and powerful, and they fought desperately. Stark was bruised and bleeding from a cut mouth before he could get in a finishing blow.

Someone rushed past him into the doorway. Treon yelled. Out of the tail of his eyes Stark saw the Lhari sitting dazed on the ground. The door was closing.

Stark hunched up his shoulders and sprang.

He hit the heavy panel with a jar that nearly knocked him breathless. It slammed open, and there was a cry of pain and the sound of someone falling. Stark burst through, to find the last of the guards rolling every which way over the floor. But one rolled over onto his feet again, drawing his sword as he rose. He had not had time before.

Stark continued his rush without stopping. He plunged headlong into the man before the point was clear of the scabbard, bore him over and down, and finished the man off with savage efficiency.

He leaped to his feet, breathing hard, spitting blood out of his mouth, and looked around the control room. But the others had fled, obviously to raise the warning.

The mechanism was simple. It was contained in a large black metal oblong about the size and shape of a coffin, equipped with grids and lenses and dials. It hummed softly to itself, but what its source of power was Stark did not know. Perhaps those same cosmic rays, harnessed to a different use.

He closed what seemed to be a master switch, and the humming stopped, and the flickering light died out of the lenses. He picked up the slain guard's sword and carefully wrecked everything that was breakable. Then he went outside again.

Treon was standing up, shaking his head. He smiled ruefully.

"It seems that strength alone is not enough," he said. "One must have skill as well."

"The barriers are down," said Stark. "The way is clear."

Treon nodded, and went with him back into the sea. This time both carried shock weapons taken from the guards—six in all, with Egil's. Total armament for war.

As they forged swiftly through the red depths, Stark asked, "What of the people of Shuruun? How will they fight?"

Treon answered, "Those of Malthor's breed will stand for the Lhari. They must, for all their hope is there. The others will wait, until they see which side is safest. They would rise against the Lhari if they dared, for we have brought them only fear in their lifetimes. But they will wait, and see."

Stark nodded. He did not speak again.

They passed over the brooding city, and Stark thought of Egil and of Malthor who were part of that silence now, drifting slowly through the empty streets where the little currents took them, wrapped in their shrouds of dim fire.

He thought of Zareth sleeping in the hall of kings, and his eyes held a cold, cruel light.

They swooped down over the slave barracks. Treon remained on watch outside. Stark went in, taking with him the extra weapons.

The slaves still slept. Some of them dreamed, and moaned in their dreaming, and others might have been dead, with their hollow faces white as skulls.

Slaves. One hundred and four, counting the women.

Stark shouted out to them, and they woke, starting up on their pallets, their eyes full of terror. Then they saw who it was that called them, standing collarless and armed, and there was a great surging and a clamor that stilled as Stark shouted again, demanding silence. This time Helvi's voice echoed his. The tall barbarian had wakened from his drugged sleep.

Stark told them, very briefly, all that happened.

"You are freed from the collar," he said. "This day you can survive or die as men, and not slaves." He paused, then asked, "Who will go with me into Shuruun?"

They answered with one voice, the voice of the Lost Ones, who saw the red pall of death begin to lift from over them. The Lost Ones, who had found hope again.

Stark laughed. He was happy. He gave the extra weapons to Helvi and three others that he chose, and Helvi looked into his eyes and laughed too.

Treon spoke from the open door. "They are coming!"

Stark gave Helvi quick instructions and darted out, taking with him one of the other men. With Treon, they hid among the shrubbery of the garden that was outside the hall, patterned and beautiful, swaying its lifeless brilliance in the lazy drifts of lire.

The guards came. Twenty of them, tall armed men, to turn out the slaves for another period of labor, dragging the useless stones.

And the hidden weapons spoke with their silent tongues.

Eight of the guards fell inside the hall. Nine of them went down outside. Ten of the slaves died before the remaining three were overcome.

Now there were twenty swords among ninety-four slaves, counting the women.

They left the city and rose up over the dreaming forest, a flight of white ghosts with flames in their hair, coming back from the red dusk and the silence to find the light again.

Light, and vengeance.

The first pale glimmer of dawn was sifting through the clouds as they came up among the rocks below the castle of the Lhari. Stark left them and went like a shadow up the tumbled cliffs to where he had hidden his gun on the night he had first come to Shuruun. Nothing stirred. The fog lifted up from the sea like a vapor of blood, and the face of Venus was still dark. Only the high clouds were touched with pearl.

Stark returned to the others. He gave one of his shock-weapons to a swamp-lander with a cold madness in his eyes. Then he spoke a few final words to Helvi and went back with Treon under the surface of the sea.

Treon led the way. He went along the face of the submerged cliff, and presently he touched Stark's arm and pointed to where a round mouth opened in the rock.

"It was made long ago," said Treon, "so that the Lhari and their slavers might come and go and not be seen. Come—and be very quiet."

They swam into the tunnel mouth, and down the dark way that lay beyond, until the lift of the floor brought them out of the sea. Then they felt their way silently along, stopping now and again to listen.

Surprise was their only hope. Treon had said that with the two of them they might succeed. More men would surely be discovered, and meet a swift end at the hands of the guards.

Stark hoped Treon was right.

They came to a blank wall of dressed stone. Treon leaned his weight against one side, and a great block swung slowly around on a central pivot. Guttering torchlight came through the crack. By it Stark could see that the room beyond was empty.

They stepped through, and as they did so a servant in bright silks came yawning into the room with a fresh torch to replace the one that was dying.

He stopped in mid-step, his eyes widening. He dropped the torch. His mouth opened to shape a scream, but no sound came, and

Stark remembered that these servants were tongueless—to prevent them from telling what they saw or heard in the castle, Treon said.

The man spun about and fled, down a long dim-lit hall. Stark ran him down without effort. He struck once with the barrel of bis gun, and the man fell and was still.

Treon came up. His face had a look almost of exaltation, a queer shining of the eyes that made Stark shiver. He led on, through a series of empty rooms, all somber black, and they met no one else for a while.

He stopped at last before a small door of burnished gold. He looked at Stark once, and nodded, and thrust the panels open and stepped through.

XII

THEY STOOD INSIDE THE VAST ECHOING HALL THAT STRETCHED away into darkness until it seemed there was no end to it. The cluster of silver lamps burned as before, and within their circle of radiance the Lhari started up from their places and stared at the strangers who had come in through their private door.

Cond, and Arel with her hands idle in her lap. Bor, pummeling the little dragon to make it hiss and snap, laughing at its impotence. Varra, stroking the winged creature on her wrist, testing with her white finger the sharpness of its beak. And the old woman, with a scrap of fat meat halfway to her mouth.

They had stopped, frozen, in the midst of these actions. And Treon walked slowly into the light.

"Do you know me?" he said.

A strange shivering ran through them. Now, as before, the old woman spoke first, her eyes glittering with a look as rapacious as her appetite.

"You are Treon," she said, and her whole vast body shook.

The name went crying and whispering off around the dark walls. Treon! Treon! Treon! Cond leaped forward, touching his cousin's straight strong body with hands that trembled.

"You have found it," he said. "The secret."

"Yes." Treon lifted his silver head and laughed, a beautiful ringing bell-note that sang from the echoing corners. "I found it, and it's gone, smashed, beyond your reach forever. Egil is dead, and the day of the Lhari is done."

There was a long, long silence, and then the old woman whispered, "You lie!"

Treon turned to Stark.

"Ask him, the stranger who came bearing doom upon his forehead. Ask him if I lie."

Cond's face became something less than human. He made a queer crazed sound and flung himself at Treon's throat.

Bor screamed suddenly. He alone was not much concerned with the finding or the losing of the secret, and he alone seemed to realize the significance of Stark's presence. He screamed, looking at the big dark man, and went rushing off down the hall, crying for the guard as he went, and the echoes roared and racketed. He fought open the great doors and ran out, and as he did so the sound of fighting came through from the compound.

The slaves, with their swords and clubs, with their stones and shards of rock, had come over the wall from the cliffs.

Stark had moved forward, but Treon did not need his help. He had got his hands around Cond's throat, and he was smiling. Stark did not disturb him.

The old woman was talking, cursing, commanding, choking on her own apoplectic breath. Arel began to laugh. She did not move, and her hands remained limp and open in her lap. She laughed and laughed, and Varra looked at Stark and hated him.

"You're a fool, wild man," she said. "You would not take what I offered you, so you shall have nothing—only death."

She slipped the hood from her creature and set it straight at Stark. Then she drew a knife from her girdle and plunged it into Treon's side.

Treon reeled back. His grip loosened and Cond tore away, half throttled, raging, his mouth flecked with foam. He drew his short sword and staggered in upon Treon.

Furious wings beat and thundered around Stark's head, and talons were clawing for his eyes. He reached up with his left hand and caught the brute by one leg and held it. Not long, but long enough to get one clear shot at Cond that dropped him in his tracks. Then he snapped the falcon's neck.

He flung the creature at Varra's feet, and picked up the gun again. The guards were rushing into the hall now at the lower end, and he began to fire at them.

Treon was sitting on the floor. Blood was coming in a steady trickle from his side, but he had the shock-weapon in his hands, and he was still smiling.

There was a great boiling roar of noise from outside. Men were fighting there, killing, dying, screaming their triumph or their pain. The echoes raged within the hall, and the noise of Stark's gun was like a hissing thunder. The guards, armed only with swords, went down like ripe wheat before the sickle, but there were many of them, too many for Stark and Treon to hold for long.

The old woman shrieked and shrieked, and was suddenly still.

Helvi burst in through the press, with a knot of collared slaves. The fight dissolved into a whirling chaos. Stark threw his gun away. He was afraid now of hitting his own men. He caught up a sword from a fallen guard and began to hew his way to the barbarian.

Suddenly Treon cried his name. He leaped aside, away from the man he was fighting, and saw Varra fall with the dagger still in her hand. She had come up behind him to stab, and Treon had seen and pressed the trigger stud just in time.

For the first time, there were tears in Treon's eyes.

A sort of sickness came over Stark. There was something horrible in this spectacle of a family destroying itself. He was too much the savage to be sentimental over Varra, but all the same he could not bear to look at Treon for a while.

Presently he found himself back to back with Helvi, and as they swung their swords—the shock-weapons had been discarded for the same reason as Stark's gun—Helvi panted, "It has been a good fight, my brother! We cannot win, but we can have a good death, which is better than slavery!"

It looked as though Helvi was right. The slaves, unfortunately, weakened by their long confinement, worn out by overwork, were being beaten back. The tide turned, and Stark was swept with it out into the compound, fighting stubbornly.

The great gate stood open. Beyond it stood the people of Shuruun, watching, hanging back—as Treon had said, they would wait and see.

In the forefront, leaning on his stick, stood Larrabee the Earthman.

Stark cut his way free of the press. He leaped up onto the wall and stood there, breathing hard, sweating, bloody, with a dripping sword in his hand. He waved it, shouting down to the men of Shuruun.

"What are you waiting for, you scuts, you women? The Lhari are dead, the Lost Ones are freed—must we of Earth do all your work for you?"

And he looked straight at Larrabee.

Larrabee stared back, his dark suffering eyes full of a bitter mirth. "Oh, well," he said in English. "Why not?"

He threw back his head and laughed, and the bitterness was gone. He voiced a high, shrill rebel yell and lifted his stick like a cudgel, limping toward the gate, and the men of Shuruun gave tongue and followed him.

After that, it was soon over.

They found Bor's body in the stable pens, where he had fled to hide when the fighting started. The dragons, maddened by the smell of the blood, had slain him very quickly.

Helvi had come through alive, and Larrabee, who had kept himself carefully out of harm's way after he had started the men of Shurrun on their attack. Nearly half the slaves were dead, and the rest wounded. Of those who had served the Lhari, few were left.

Stark went back into the great hall. He walked slowly, for he was very weary, and where he set his foot there was a bloody print, and his arms were red to the elbows, and his breast was splashed with the redness. Treon watched him come, and smiled, nodding.

"It is as I said. And I have outlived them all."

Arel had stopped laughing at last. She had made no move to run away, and the tide of battle had rolled over her and drowned her unaware. The old woman lay still, a mountain of inert flesh upon her bed. Her hand still clutched a ripe fruit, clutched convulsively in the moment of death, the red juice dripping through her fingers.

"Now I am going, too," said Treon, "and I am well content. With me goes the last of our rotten blood, and Venus will be the cleaner for it. Bury my body deep, stranger with the fierce eyes. I would not have it looked on after this."

He sighed and fell forward.

Bor's little dragon crept whimpering out from its hiding place under the old woman's bed and scurried away down the hall, trailing its dragging rope.

舌

Stark leaned on the taffrail, watching the dark mass of Shuruun recede into the red mists.

The decks were crowded with the outland slaves, going home. The Lhari were gone, the Lost Ones freed forever, and Shuruun was now only another port on the Red Sea. Its people would still be wolf's-heads and pirates, but that was natural and as it should be. The black evil was gone.

Stark was glad to see the last of it. He would be glad also to see the last of the Red Sea.

The off-shore wind sent the ship briskly down the gulf. Stark thought of Larrabee, left behind with his dreams of winter snows and city streets and women with dainty feet. It seemed that he had lived too long in Shuruun, and had lost the courage to leave it.

"Poor Larrabee," he said to Helvi, who was standing near him. "He'll die in the mud, still cursing it."

80

Someone laughed behind him. He heard a limping step on the deck and turned to see Larrabee coming toward him.

"Changed my mind at the last minute," Larrabee said. 'Tve been below, lest I should see my muddy brats and be tempted to change it again." He leaned beside Stark, shaking his head. "Ah, well, they'll do nicely without me. I'm an old man, and I've a right to choose my own place to die in. I'm going back to Earth, with you."

Stark glanced at him. "I'm not going to Earth."

Larrabee sighed. "No. No, I suppose you're not. After all, you're no Earthman, really, except for an accident of blood. Where are you going?"

"I don't know. Away from Venus, but I don't know yet where."

Larrabee's dark eyes surveyed him shrewdly. " 'A restless, cold-eyed tiger of a man,' that's what Varra said. He's lost something, she said. He'll look for it all his life, and never find it."

After that there was silence. The red fog wrapped them, and the wind rose and sent them scudding before it.

Then, faint and far off, there came a moaning wail, a sound like broken chanting that turned Stark's flesh cold.

All on board heard it. They listened, utterly silent, their eyes wide, and somewhere a woman began to weep.

Stark shook himself. "It's only the wind," he said roughly, "in the rocks by the strait."

The sound rose and fell, weary, infinitely mournful, and the part of Stark that was N'Chaka said that he lied. It was not the wind that keened so sadly through the mists. It was the voices of the Lost Ones who were forever lost—Zareth, sleeping in the hall of kings, and all the others who would never leave the dreaming city and the forest, never find the light again.

Stark shivered, and turned away, watching the leaping fires of the strait sweep toward them.

THE END

About the Author

Leigh Douglass Brackett was born December 7th, 1915 in Los Angeles, California. Considered the 'Queen of Space Opera', Brackett was first published in her mid-20s in *Astounding Science Fiction* and was very prolific from the outset. She wrote in different genres; her novel *No Good From a Corpse*, a hard-boiled mystery, led to the second phase of her writing career as a screenwriter, working with William Faulkner on *The Big Sleep*. She married writer Edmond Hamilton in 1946, and the couple nurtured and inspired each other, establishing two strong and entirely separate careers in science fiction writing.

Returning to SF in the '50s, Brackett's planetary adventures grew in length and complexity, as in *The Sea-Kings of Mars*. Brackett's greatest creation of that era was Eric John Stark, an earthman raised on Mercury, who proceeds to have adventures across the solar system. His first apprearance was in *Queen of the Martian Catacombs*.

She returned to TV and film writing in the '60s and '70s, penning westerns starring John Wayne, and Robert Altman's adaptation of Raymond Chandler's *The Long Goodbye*, and the first draft of *The Empire Strikes Back*, which was to be her last work before dying from cancer in 1978.

Leigh Brackett was a pioneer for women in the genre, often unchallenged for her writing. The skill, intricacy, & diversity of her writing projects established an admiration and acceptance among her peers that many women writers struggled to achieve.

OTHER BOOKS BY VERTVOLTA PRESS

THE NIGHT OF THE LONG KNIVES, by Fritz Leiber
978-1-60944-112-8, $9.99

PIONEER DAYS ON PUGET SOUND, by Arthur A. Denny
978-1-60944-051-0, $11.00

VANCOUVER'S DISCOVERY OF PUGET SOUND: *Portraits and Biographies of the Men Honored in the Naming of Geographic Features of Northwestern America,* by Edmond S. Meany
978-1-60944-126-5, $16.99

D'ORCY'S AIRSHIP MANUAL: *An International Register of Airships With A Compendium of the Airship's Elementary Mechanics,* by Baron Ladislas D'Orcy
978-1-60944-126-5, $19.95

BE VIGILANT, BUT NOT AFRAID: The Farewell Speeches of BARACK OBAMA *44th President of the United State of America and* MICHELLE OBAMA *Former First Lady of the United States of America.*
978-1-60944-111-1, $9.00

ANARCHISM AND OTHER ESSAYS, by EMMA GOLDMAN
978-1-60944-113-5, $14.00

FLY TO THE ASSEMBLIES: *Seattle and the Rise of the Resistance* edited by MARCUS HARRISON GREEN
978-1-60944-116-6, $15.99

EMERALD REFLECTIONS: *A South Seattle Emerald Anthology* edited by MARCUS HARRISON GREEN
978-1-60944-109-8, $17.00

www.ingramcontent.com/pod-product-compliance
Lightning Source LLC
Chambersburg PA
CBHW030417120726
47904CB00007B/2314